ALIEN ABDUCTION

LEE SAVINO

GOLDEN ANGEL

ALIEN ABDUCTION

This Tsenturion warrior has waited a thousand years for a mate, and nothing will stop him from claiming me.

I was dying, but now I'm fine. My e-reader sucked me through to another universe, where I'm healed and being trained as an alien bride. Don't get me wrong, I'm grateful for the new chance at life, but I'm not sure I want to be mated to a hulking, brooding, bossy alien.

Though he's kinda hard to resist...

Relationship status between me and my giant alien abductor: **it's complicated.**

Alien Abduction is a hot alien warrior romance, starring one stubborn human and the Tsenturion warrior strong enough to master her.

Disclaimer: the authors are not responsible for any actual alien abductions that may result should you purchase this book. ;)

CHAPTER 1

*M*arta
   I'm alive.

I shouldn't be.

The last thing I remember is my e-reader blinking at me, and half my body being buried under a pile of rubble after a bomb went off. I'd been bleeding out. I'd been dying but now I'm alive. Unless... am I supposed to be heading toward the bright light?

I blink but the light above me remains the same. It appears to be mechanical and not the bright light of heaven drawing me in.

"Hello, Marta Flores Romero, please do not panic." The deep voice from off to the side startles me, but I don't panic. Mostly. My brain immediately starts going to work, picking up clues. Male voice, deep, and with an almost pleading note to it.

"Uh, okay. Panicking isn't really my thing anyway." I start to try to sit up and my heart flutters when I realize I'm tied down. Okay, the whole 'don't panic' thing makes a lot more sense now. I bite my lip.

I will *not* panic. I'm not dead, but there are also things worse than death. All the reasons why I might be tied down to whatever I'm lying on flit through my head, and none of them are good.

"I am pleased to hear that. Please remain calm, and I will remove the restraints."

Okay, that's marginally reassuring. I try to look towards the voice—even my head is strapped down to the table—and I can see some movement in the darker area of the room, but I can't see who the voice belongs to.

"Is there a reason for the restraints?" *Keep it conversational. Don't show panic if he doesn't want you to panic. You can do this.*

"Previous representatives of your species have proven difficult when making the transition from Earth to here."

That's ominous. What does he mean, *representatives of my species?*

"Where is 'here' exactly? And who are you?" I squint at the darker section of the room, trying to see if the speaker is hiding there.

The straps slide away from my wrists, ankles, torso, and head all at once, freeing me entirely. I lift my head, staring down at myself for a moment, before sitting straight up. It's only then that I realize I'm uninjured. Completely. The lower half of my body, which had been crushed, is in perfect condition.

I can see that because I'm naked except for a pair of black panties that fit me perfectly. Smooth, unblemished, bronze skin, and not a single injury that would account for all the blood loss.

I stare at myself in shock before remembering and jerking my head around to find the source of the voice. I was right—he was hiding out in the shadows, but it's not a 'he', it's an 'it.' Literally an 'it.'

A large blob of Jello wobbles forward into the light. It's tall enough to come up to my shoulder, but that's exactly what it looks like, Jello. Or maybe tapioca pudding, because of the color. I don't feel remotely hungry looking at it though. There's something a little nauseating about watching it move.

Panic bubbles up in the back of my throat, even though I said it wouldn't.

This is the freakiest thing that's ever happened to me, and I haven't exactly lived a quiet life.

It's not like I can control my emotions, but I can control how much I let them show. The good news is that I'm used to crazy situations. And I have an amazing poker face. I push the panic away, knowing that it won't help me right now. And I promised I wouldn't.

Besides, there's no reason to panic just because I woke up naked and healed in a strange place with a moving blob of Jello. Yup. No reason at all. Waking up with the cartel would be far worse, right?

"My name is Frllil. I am a Jabols Luminary. You are located in my ex-planetary lab on the third moon of the eighth planet in the Jabolian system." The voice is definitely coming from the blob. I stare at it. How is it talking? There's no opening that looks like a mouth, nothing that would indicate it has vocal chords, but there's no doubt it's speaking to me.

There's also no doubt what it is.

"You're an alien."

"That is the word you would use to describe me, yes."

My brain is finally catching up, and is suddenly going a million miles a minute. *Holy shit, aliens! Aliens are real! This is the story of a lifetime!* Except... except I'm in his lab, located on the third moon of the eighth planet in the Jabolian system, which means absolutely nothing to me, but I sincerely doubt it's anywhere near Earth. The urge to call my boss subsides.

"And why am I here?" The question pops out of my mouth. In every sci-fi book I've ever read, there are only three options for what the aliens want: to conquer Earth, to experiment on humans, or to mate with us. I've read a lot about that last option, but I am having trouble believing that I'm genetically compatible with extra shiny tapioca pudding.

"You are here to undergo the training necessary to become the Tribute to a Tsenturion warrior." Something about the words triggers a memory in the back of my brain. Didn't I read some books about Tsenturions?

Hm. Maybe this is a hallucination... but I've had hallucinations before. The most vivid ones were during a spirit quest with a tribe I was writing a story about, and even then I knew that they weren't real. This—despite everything—feels real.

"Yeah, I'm gonna need a little more than that, because none of those words made sense together." I cross my arms over my chest and glare at Frllil, hoping I look threatening. Can Jello be threatened? I mean, seriously, what am I going to do if he doesn't answer me? I'm not even sure he has bones, though there have got to be some kind of internal organs, right?

Thankfully, he starts talking. I can't tell if he's intimidated or not, but I'm guessing 'not.'

It turns out the little bit I remember from the Tsenturion books was right—there's another alien species (not Frllil's) and they need compatible mates. And humans are a match. Even though I should probably be freaking out, I mostly feel excited. The panic has receded, and the astounding nature of my current position is really hitting home.

This is... this is incredible. I am talking to an actual alien. How many humans can say they've done that?

Well, now that I know aliens are real, maybe a few more than I would think, because who knows how many true stories have been dismissed as lies, but still. *They're real! They exist!* And they saved my life. At least, Frllil did. And I am very happy to be alive.

Frllil explains to me about the Tsenturion Warriors and *why* they need human females. I hear about the loss of their entire planet at the hands of another group of aliens called the Vgotha and how they became allies with Frllil's race, the Jabols. The Jabols were also persecuted by the Vgotha until they made contact with the Tsenturions. Now the two work together, combining the Jabols' technology and the Tsenturions' military expertise, to remove the threat to the universe.

All my journalist instincts are tingling by the time he's done talking. Not that anyone back on Earth would care about something that's going on light years away, but man… what a story. And it's kinda nice to know that it's not just Earth that has all sorts of violent and fucked up situations going on.

Not that I'd wish harm to others, but somehow I always imagined other aliens looking at us from afar, seeing all our wars and bigotry and the disdainful way some people are treated, and thinking, 'Nope. Not gonna touch that.' To know they have their own problems is somehow comforting. Like, maybe I've been abducted and moved halfway across the universe, but how fucked up people can be to each other… well, that's something I'm familiar with, and apparently it transcends species.

Sad, but familiar. That's a good description.

"Okay, so, you're going to train me to be a good little alien bride, and… what do I get out of this, again?" I eye Frllil a little dubiously. Granted, he's got me dressed for the part, but he seems to be missing some of the necessary equipment. He's a blobby little thing, and not at all arousing to look at.

"You get to live," Frllil replies, and his words hit me like a punch to the gut. "I saved your life. You would be dead right now if not for me."

Oh, okay. It's a debt, he's not actually threatening my life. I think.

"So, you're saying I owe you?" I ask, just to confirm. Debt is something I'm familiar with, and I do have my own sense of honor. On the other hand, giving up the entire rest of my life—an especially long life, according to Frllil, since my biology has been changed to match a Tsenturion's—seems a little demanding.

"If that inspires your cooperation." Since he doesn't have a face, it's kind of hard to pinpoint exactly how he feels about it.

"What happens if I don't cooperate?" I ask. Rather than getting a verbal answer, after a moment, something hits me right in my clit.

I don't mean that metaphorically. It's like a zap of electricity right on the most sensitive part of my body and makes me double over and gasp for breath, both hands over the panties. Except... they aren't panties. I can't shift them away from my body at all. I can't even feel my clit, and my clit can't feel my fingers. The panic that had receded is starting to come back, because holy fuck, that hurt like nothing I've ever experienced before.

Who electrocutes someone in the clit?!

And then the not-panties start to hum. The vibration is soothing for a moment and then it begins to grow. I moan, my thighs trembling, both of my hands pressed over the front of the panties—but I have no control. The acute pain has morphed into hot pleasure as all my most sensitive bits tingle and buzz. I press my hands against the not-panties, trying to find the edges, to pull them away as the sensory overload begins to swamp me, but there's not even the tiniest gap for my fingers to slip under.

"Stop it… I get it…" I gasp out the words as the vibrations climb higher. My nipples perk up, swollen and aching as the rest of my body careens towards orgasm. But I don't want to come in front of Frllil. I don't want to be that vulnerable in front of him. I don't want to be vulnerable at all—no matter what, I've always had control of my body and my reactions, but now he's controlling me, and it's terrifying.

To my shock and relief, the vibration stops. I'm only relieved for a moment, though, and then I feel like whimpering, because even though the vibration stopped, I am so close to orgasm that the need to finish the job is so strong, it's painful. My fingers are still pressing down on the not-panties, right over my clit, trying to rub… but I can't feel it at all.

I bite back a curse. My entire body is throbbing painfully.

"Good." Frllil sounds pleased, the fucker. "We will begin with your priming now."

My priming?

The vibration begins again, much lower than before, a tease that will not bring me the orgasm my body now craves.

"Come over here," Frllil says, blopping along towards one of the walls, which suddenly turns into a screen. I manage to scramble off the table and follow him, biting my lip against the low hum that flutters against my pussy, continuing to tease me. On the screen, an incredible hunk of muscle and sex appeal appears.

He has golden skin that actually shimmers, a humanoid body and facial features, and muscles upon muscles upon muscles. My jaw drops. Even without the weird panties, I feel like my clit might be humming after seeing this guy.

"This is Commander Arkdhem, third-in-command of the remaining Tsenturions. You are his Tribute. The High

Commander and Commander Bogdan, the second-in-command, have already received their Tributes: Dawn Cahill, and Dr. Pareena Singh."

My jaw drops. Other human women?

Actually, that's encouraging. It must have been scary as hell being the first person to be taken by these aliens. Knowing that two others have come before me and lived to tell the tale is reassuring.

As he wraps up his explanation of how I'll be mated to Commander Arkdhem and that it's Frllil's job to 'prime' me for that mating, the pile of Jello focuses back on me. How I can tell he's doing so when he's a blob, I don't know, don't ask me to explain, but I can feel it.

"You are certainly the calmest and most agreeable of the Tributes so far," he says, sounding pleased.

Is it weird to feel good about that? I've always had a bit of a competitive streak. I'm the best at being calm after being abducted by aliens? Cool. Though it does make me wonder what their reactions were. Screaming? Fighting? Maybe he didn't save their lives. It tends to put things into perspective.

Still, these not-panties are now driving me a little crazy and I'm feeling a lot less agreeable, but I can fake it for a while longer. At least until I've had more time to figure out my situation, and whether or not there's anything I can actually do about it. Right now, I'm completely at Frllil's mercy, and I know it.

"I'm here now. Like you said, you saved my life. I didn't want to die and now that I'm here, well, might as well make the most of the situation. Besides, I've read a lot of books about sexy aliens, and had a lot of fantasies about it. Now I'm supposed to argue when one of my fantasies is coming to life?" I sound more agreeable than I'm actually feeling, but there's a lot of truth to what I'm saying too.

And the more the vibrations hum against my needy

pussy, the more I'm interested in having that particular fantasy fulfilled.

Maybe I should be freaking out more, but all my life, I've rolled with the punches. Why stop now?

"That is exactly why we provided that book," Frllil says, sounding even more pleased. "The purpose was to identify females who would be agreeable to being part of the Tribute Program."

Oh. *Oh*. So it was my reading habits that got me into this. That... actually makes a lot of sense.

"Cool, tell me more," I say, doing my best to ignore the way my pussy is humming. I squirm, trying to find a way to relieve some of the pressure—or add some—but apparently, these are magic panties, and I can't quite figure out how to make them work for me. The best I'm going to be able to do is try and distract myself.

If I learn more about Frllil and his tech, maybe I can find a way to make the panties less frustrating—or even get them off of myself.

* * *

BY DAY Three of being cooped up with Frllil, I'm ready to scream from sexual frustration. Being 'primed' is bullshit. Especially for this long. The vibrating panties—aka 'Bride Trainer'—are a torture device, I'm convinced of it.

Not that I'll ever admit to a weakness, so I do my best to ignore it and instead try to distract myself by asking Frllil a million questions about his work, his tech, the Jabol culture, Dawn and Pareena... the stuff that won't turn me on the way just thinking about a Tsenturion warrior now does.

Yeah, not going to think about Arkdhem. Because being primed means being constantly aroused with no completion.

It's orgasm torture of the highest form, and it sucks *burro* balls.

Still, my priming seems a lot easier than what Dawn Cahill went through. Reading the files on her training as the first Tribute, I am very glad that the training process changed after her. Thanks to her. Whatever. Getting stuck with needles full of an aphrodisiac sounds awful. The nanotech belt is bad enough—and at least it has some upsides, like being self-cleaning and taking care of my 'waste.'

I'm spending my days with Frllil, who is trying to make me focus on what a good little Tsenturion mate is supposed to do—be ready and willing to have sex, as far as I can tell—while I attempt to distract him with all my questions. He seems to find my thirst for knowledge commendable. Since he can't spend all his time with me, he gives me access to the archives and, once he's shown me how to use the Jabolian equivalent of a computer, I spend my free time searching through them and trying to ignore the state of my needy vagina. And, honestly, other than the incessant sexual arousal, it's not a bad way to spend my time.

I'm learning about real life freaking aliens! God, if I ever get back to Earth, I'm so writing a book. It will probably have to be fiction, unless I can bring some proof with me, but who cares? It'd be one hell of a book, and hopefully informative for any other poor woman who gets sucked through her e-reader to be a Tribute.

My chances of getting back to Earth seem pretty slim, but hey, a girl can dream.

There's a lot of information about the Tsenturions—their customs, and how they lived before their planet was destroyed by the Vgotha. Their alliance with the Jabol. Jabolian culture—which seems to be mostly focused on the gathering of scientific data and research, as well as making a study of other alien species. I look, but there's very little about the Vgotha. The number of unknowns make them seem even more threatening.

There's a lot about Earth, though, and the other two human females who came here before me. Dawn Cahill and Dr. Pareena Singh. There are pictures too, which are reassuring. Both of them are beautiful, but within the normal range. They aren't supermodels or anything, which means that Arkdhem shouldn't be disappointed with me.

And why do you care if he's disappointed with you?

Shut it, I tell the little voice in my head. Sometimes my competitive streak can take over and I know it, but I don't need to compete with these women for looks. Also, I'm being brainwashed by Frllil into caring.

But I can't even be mad at Frllil. He's just doing his job, and he's not doing me any harm, other than not letting me orgasm. Otherwise, he's a very lenient alien abductor.

And I can't forget that I could be dead right now. *Should* be dead. I was dying, and I wasn't going to be able to do any more good or help inspire any more changes until he saved me. No, I'm not going to be able to make my mark on my world anymore, but maybe I can make my mark on their world, the Tsenturion's world. And as more than a breeder, that is absolutely something I'm determined to do.

Frllil says Arkdhem is the third in command of the remaining Tsenturions, so he's highly placed in their society. I can see where Dawn, the High Commander's Tribute, has already changed the Tribute Program. Unlike me, she wasn't dying when she was sucked through her e-reader. She'd had a life, she'd had a future, and so she fought to change things for the Tributes who came after her.

I can do that too.

Maybe I was thinking too small when I wanted to change the world. Now, I have a chance to change the universe.

CHAPTER 2

a<u>*rkdhem*</u>

    The closer the ship gets to Frllil's lab, the farther I am from the Tsenturion fleet and my duty. A small thread of guilt over disobeying the High Commander's orders has sunk into my very bones, but I do not let it distract me from my self-assigned mission.

Not only is the Tribute *my* Tribute, but if, as the High Commander believes, the Jabol are the ones who destroyed our planet and not the Vgotha, then she is in danger. Still, I know there will be a price to pay upon my return. I could have contacted the High Commander and interrupted his honeymoon, or even waited for him and Dawn, his Tribute, to return. But I did neither because I did not trust that he would agree to retrieve her.

Not with the anger that he has towards the Jabol right now, after uncovering their supposed perfidy.

I am still unsure whether I believe the Vgotha's account, or the vid they showed us of the Jabol destroying Tsentur, but either way, I cannot leave a Tribute—*my* Tribute, my heart—in their hands. I will take whatever punishment the

High Commander deems necessary when I return, as long as she is safe. Whether or not the Jabol are our true enemy is irrelevant when it comes to her.

"Commander Arkdhem, we are approaching," Vardill says, looking up from his screen. Sitting in the Command Chair in the center of the bridge, I nod, unable to keep my armor from flashing gold and announcing my happiness, or the smile from curving my lips. I do not care about the show of emotion, though—what warrior would not feel the same when confronted with the imminent joining with his mate? Certainly, none of the other warriors seem surprised. They look at me with a mixture of hope and envy, each one wishing to be the next to receive their own Tribute.

"Open a channel to Frllil to announce our arrival." My heart races in my chest, my hands gripping the ends of the arm rests more tightly. Soon, I will be able to touch her. Hold her. Worship her.

My Tribute.

* * *

Marta

If I'd thought the not-panties—I still refuse to call them a Bride Trainer so they're vibrating not-panties as far as I'm concerned—were annoying on a low hum, they are so, so much worse on their current setting. My pussy lips buzz, but no matter how I shift, I can't get the humming vibrations to touch my needy, swollen clit.

I just want to get off!

"Their ship has arrived," Frllil says, sounding a little anxious as he escorts me to the pod I'll be taking to the claiming ceremony. "Are you ready?"

"Ready." I smile at him, ignoring my frustration with both him and the panties. One thing I've learned about Frllil and the Jabolian society as I've been here is that they're very duty-conscious. He's doing the job that he was assigned to do, and even though it's sexual torture for me, it's not personal on his part.

I can see why that pissed off the previous Tributes—especially Dawn Cahill, apparently—but I try to be nice to Frllil anyway. We've formed a sort of friendship, the kind that I haven't had in years, thanks to my work. Maybe it's from proximity to each other, but I truly believe he's at least a little fond of me, and as for me... well, it's hard to admit but I'm actually kind of attached to the blobby guy.

My dad had always taught me not to get involved in situations as a journalist. We're supposed to be the outside observer, watching but not part of it, but that hasn't been possible here. Besides, new planet, new rules. My mom would be happy that I made a friend, even if it is a blobby alien who's training me to become the breeding mate for a different alien.

Hmm. On second thought, she might not be so happy about that part, but she'd be happy about the friend thing.

"Are you going to walk me down the aisle?" I ask, teasing. A little pang hits my heart. I'd never expected to get married back on Earth. I'd always been more married to my job, but when I was a little girl, I'd always assumed my dad would fulfill that duty. A wave of grief and longing passes over me. I miss him so much... but I push the emotion aside. I barely cried when my dad and mom died, I'm not going to break down now. It won't be helpful to my current situation.

If Frllil had eyes, I bet he'd have blinked. Instead, he pauses a moment, as if considering my request.

"I may accompany you, if you wish. It would be highly irregular, but there is no protocol against it." He still sounds hesitant, though, and I shake my head.

"It's okay, Frllil. I was just trying to lighten the mood." I've done most things in my life on my own, why would this be any different? Besides, Dawn and Pareena both went to their Claiming ceremonies alone. I can, too. "I'm a big girl, I'll be fine."

It's not like it's going to be that hard. I arrive, walk down the aisle past the rows of Tsenturion warriors, and meet Arkdhem for the first time. My big alien hottie. He'll look me over and give me some kind of ceremonial first touch, and then he'll take me back to his quarters to claim me.

My body hums in anticipation, ready to reach some kind of climax. Anything to make this incessant ache between my legs cease. At this point, I'd probably be ready to mate with Frllil if that was my only option, just to make the hot need go away for a little while. The fact that the only being who is supposed to get me off is a super hot, big, golden alien with muscles upon muscles is not the worst thing in the universe.

Fulfill my physical needs now. Figure out the rest later. It's basically how I've lived most of my life, even if I've never done anything quite like this.

Don't forget, the big guy really only wants you for breeding.

Yeah, yeah. That's a problem for future Marta, and only if I get pregnant. According to Frllil's notes, the Tsenturions have not reported anything about the other two Tributes conceiving yet—and Dawn was mated to the High Commander months ago—so I'm not super worried. I should have time to figure things out.

And until then, no-holds-barred kinky sex with Arkdhem sounds great. After a thousand years without sex, he's probably got a lot of energy to work off, and I am here and ready to help.

I'm certainly dressed for it, in a filmy, light purple gown that barely covers anything. My nipples are clearly visible through the material. It looks really nice against my golden brown skin and dark hair and I have to admit, I feel stunning.

"Here we are." Frlil comes to a stop outside a small oval pod. It looks big enough to hold me and maybe two other people. Good thing I'm not claustrophobic, and that the ride is short. He turns towards me. At least, that's how I interpret his movements. Since he doesn't have eyes or a face or anything, it's kind of hard to tell. "Good luck, Marta Romero Flores." He pauses, hesitating for a moment. "It has been a pleasure coming to know you."

"You too, Frlil. I'm gonna miss you." I sigh. "I have so many more questions I could ask."

There's an odd pause and then part of his blobby self extends, turning into a hand. Automatically, I reach out my hand as well, and he drops a small round object into it.

"This is a special comm unit. Put it in your ear. If you have questions or you need to contact me, press your ear closed for three of your seconds and, when I am able, I will contact you."

"In my ear?" I ask a little dubiously.

"You will not be able to feel it. And when I contact you, it will be as if I am speaking in your ear. I will be able to hear anything you say."

Okay, sure, why not. I reach up and drop it into my ear. It's the oddest sensation, as if it's rolling around and then suddenly it comes to a stop. Nothing. I poke my finger in my ear, trying to feel it, but instead of a ball, there's now a very smooth patch just inside. Nanotech is freaking amazing. This is way better than the not-panties.

"Good. It is secure," Frlil says. "Time for you to go."

"Thank you, Frlil."

I step into the pod. Time to go meet my mate and my destiny.

I would be lying if I said I'm not hoping to also get the

orgasm I'm craving. Because I'm pretty sure I'm going to go insane soon if I don't. And it's going to be hard to figure out how to make my mark on the universe if I'm distracted by my body's craving for sex.

* * *

Arkdhem

The pod containing my Tribute comes to a rest at the end of the aisle, opposite the platform I'm standing on. The ranks of warriors between it and me somehow seem far too many, when a few moments before, I had worried about there being far fewer than there were for Dawn or Pareena.

It does not matter the size of the audience. What matters is her.

The door to the pod slides open, and there she is.

Despite the distance between us, I can see how beautiful she is. Her lush curves strain the filmy gown she is wearing, and I can imagine how full and soft she will feel in my hands. The Bride Trainer is visible beneath the lavender fabric and it swirls around her legs as she walks towards me.

Her hair blows around her shoulders, the sun glinting off it, and my *seela* begin to move as my cock perks up with interest. I know from Dawn and Pareena that human males do not have *seela*. The two Tributes call them 'pube tentacles,' but neither of them seem to have any complaints. Hopefully my Tribute will not, either.

As I stare at Marta, drinking in the sight of her, I can already imagine peeling her gown off her. Knowing that everyone can see her beautiful body so clearly through the filmy gown makes me want to growl with possessiveness, but I hold my position.

The rows of warriors stare at her with both hope and reverence. Another Tribute. Another symbol of hope for our future. Marta makes three, and I am very aware how lucky I am to have her. I would never deny my fellow warriors the sight of her, no matter how it stirs my possessiveness, because I know they are not really thinking about her.

No, they are thinking about the day when they may receive a Tribute.

I can only hope that they do. If what the Vgotha say about the Jabol is true… but my mind rejects those thoughts. I need to focus on the present and the female coming toward me, not on the possible issues of the future.

Her gaze meets mine, her large, dark eyes fringed with long lashes, her pouty lips slightly parted. I can see the glazed look on her face, so similar to Dawn and Pareena's when they arrived, announcing her arousal. Plump nipples press against the shimmering fabric she wears, begging for my touch.

I grit my teeth, forcing myself to remain stoic, which is not at all easy for me. My armor is bright gold—so bright, it is practically glowing—and it is all I can do to keep myself from running down to meet her.

She reaches the ramp and walks up, her gaze locked with mine. Her breasts heave with every breath she takes, and her tongue darts out to wet her lips. I nearly groan as my cock springs fully to life despite my best efforts to remain stoic, my armor flashing brighter with my own arousal. My *seela* writhe with need, aching to latch on to her.

She is supposed to stop at the top of the ramp, she is supposed to wait for me to come to her, but instead she suddenly lunges towards me. I automatically reach out to catch her as she leaps upon me, wrapping her legs around me, and I find myself holding an armful of female flesh for the first time in my life.

* * *

MARTA

Damn panties—or maybe it's his armor, but I can't feel anything on the spot right where I need it. The vibrations had gotten more powerful as I walked towards Arkdhem, the sexy gold alien who is supposed to finally give me some relief, and I couldn't contain myself. So I jumped on him and tried to rub my pussy against him, but the vibrations immediately ceased, denying me my orgasm, and I can't feel anything through the stupid panties.

Behind me, the ranks break out into a shouted chant, and Arkdhem laughs, his hands curving around my butt. I can feel his calluses against my skin, but—again—nothing where the panties cover me.

"My Tribute is eager," he says, chuckling and squeezing my bottom. Holy hell, that feels good. I whimper a little. I know I was supposed to wait, but fuck that. I'm a 'go-getter,' and the closer I got to him, the less I cared about what I was supposed to do.

"You have no idea," I tell him. Yeah, yeah, Frllil told me there was all this pomp and ceremony and I'm totally ruining it, but I can't bring myself to care right now. This big alien is hard and hot between my legs right now and I want to be able to *feel* him, dammit! I could scream with the sexual frustration running through me, except that it wouldn't provide any relief.

He turns to the big alien next to him, who is also as sexy and yet somehow, I don't find him as appealing as the one holding me—which is a little weird, because why should I have a preference? But maybe that's part of the conditioning Frllil did with me. Pretty much my entire 'priming' was done with me staring at pictures of Arkdhem. That's got to have some kind of effect on my psyche.

I'll worry about that later, when I've finally gotten to experience some alien peen and I'm not so damn horny.

"I will take my Tribute to my quarters to complete our joining," he says to Sexy Alien #2. "You will helm the bridge. Set a course back to the fleet."

Hands still on my ass, he turns and carries me into the ship.

Fuck yes, finally!

Peeking over his shoulder, I can see the rows of warriors breaking rank, some of them shaking their heads, as Arkdhem carries me into the ship. Oops. Oh well. He doesn't seem to mind, and that's the important thing.

CHAPTER 3

Marta

Being carried to Arkdhem's rooms is another exercise in frustration. I still can't feel him through my panties, but my nipples are stiff and rubbing against his armor. The fabric over them is textured, and they're becoming so sensitive that the constant motion and rubbing is almost painfully stimulating.

I whimper, squirming against him.

"Are you well, my heart?" Arkdhem asks as I wriggle.

"These panties are driving me nuts," I wail. Pride? Who needs pride? I don't. At least, not right now. I need to climax, and sacrifices must be made. Pride can take a hike if it'll get me off. "I can't feel anything through them."

"Soon." His deep, sexy whisper in my ear makes my heart do a funny pitter-patter, flip-flop. "My nanotech is already bonding with yours. Can you feel this?"

Mother fucker…

The spot right over my clit begins to hum harder than the rest of my panties and I shriek, rocking my hips against him and panting as the sensation swirls through me. So close, I'm so, so close—and then it fades away again.

"Fuck!"

He chuckles again and I would slap him, but then he says something that makes me feel a lot better.

"We are here." A door swooshes open behind me and I can feel his sudden rush before I'm unceremoniously dumped onto a bed.

The gown's skirt slides around my legs, and I stare up at him as he reaches down to pull it off of me. It's more of a tunic with some rope to hold it in place than a dress, and easily slides off when he tugs at the knots holding it around my waist.

I look at his armor a little dubiously, because that looks like a lot of work to take off and I'm not sure I can wait that long, and then suddenly it melts into his skin. Holy golden humanoid, he's even more beautiful in person than he was in the pictures. I want to touch every inch of his muscled body… and maybe lick it too… except then my gaze falls to his crotch, and I can't help the small shriek that falls from my lips.

He's so humanoid in every way that, even though part of my brain was hoping for some freaky alien peen, I don't think I truly believed it would be all that different from a human male's. Boy, was I wrong.

Yeah, there's a shaft and a head, but the head doesn't look anything like a mushroom. It's got a blunt point and then flares out, almost like the shape of a stingray, and the 'wings' even flap gently up and down. I gulp, trying to imagine what that will feel like inside of me.

The rest of his shaft is thick and ridged, growing wider towards the base, and at the base where his cock meets his body is where the really freaky stuff is.

Tentacles. Lots of tiny tentacles with one particularly

long tentacle right above his cock. I've never been much into hentai but I'm suddenly wishing I'd watched a little bit more to help prepare me for this. Where do they all go? Do they go anywhere, or do they stay on the outside?

I shiver. *Two women have been through this before you, and they're okay. You can do this!*

But are they okay? I haven't actually met them yet, so how do I really know that? At some point, I need to contact Frllil and tell him that he really needs to add Alien Sex 101 to the priming curriculum because Tsenturion anatomy was not covered in the course material.

"You are well primed for me. Do not worry. I will make you feel very good." Arkdhem grips his shaft and pumps it. The little tentacles wave wildly in response. I can't take my eyes off of them. With his other hand, he cups his fingers around the writhing tentacles, clearly catching on to my interest. "These are my *seela*. They will help make you feel good too."

The panties hum to life again and I fall back against the bed. *Fuck!* My hips lift upwards, leaving me gasping. I press my hands against my pussy, but I still can't feel the pressure thanks to the damn panties. The freakiness of Arkdhem's alien peen suddenly means a lot less in the face of my overwhelming need.

* * *

Arkdhem

I can feel Marta's need thrumming through me, thanks to the nanotech. Already, we are bonding. I love seeing her squirming and writhing for me. From the way her eyes grew big, I could see that she was surprised by my *seela*, but Dawn and Pareena's discussions had prepared me for that. I am looking forward to showing her how good they can make her feel.

Kneeling on the bed, I push her legs apart, but I keep the Bride Trainer over her pussy for now, continuing to stimulate her while I run my hands up and down her limbs. Her skin is so soft. She moans, reaching down and pressing her hands over her pussy. Such a needy sound. Such a sweet, desperate female.

Leaning down, I press my lips against the skin on her pillowy thigh, just beneath the Bride Trainer, and she nearly levitates off the bed.

"Holy shit, Arkdhem!"

I like to hear my name on her lips. Turning my head, I do it again to her other leg.

"Please... just fuck me... Enough teasing, I'm dying up here!"

"No, you are not. I will not let you die. But I will pleasure you and make this special. The manuals indicated that the first joining between a male and female is very important to humans."

"Manuals?" She sounds confused, and the glazed look in her eyes makes me wonder if she's understanding everything I'm saying.

I nod at the stack of books on the table next to my bed. I have studied them every night, ever since the Tribute Program began, for when I received my own Tribute. I also added a few new ones after Frllil sent me the reading list from her 'e-reader.' Marta's eyes widen.

"Oh, my god... You have Sara Fields... and Cari Silverwood... and—is that the *Claimed Brides* anthology?" It's hard to tell exactly how she feels about the stack, but I am rather proud of them. I have read all of them cover to cover.

"Yes. I have an extensive collection of manuals from your world." The best collection of any of the Tsenturions, in fact.

Even before I met her, I was dedicated to ensuring my Tribute has the best of everything, and now that I have her, I am glad I am so well prepared.

Marta whimpers. "Those aren't... they aren't..."

"Pareena and Dawn have explained that they are fiction. I understand that every female's needs are different. I look forward to ascertaining yours." I smile at her, moving up along her body to press my lips to her soft stomach. She moans as my hands slide up her sides to her breasts, cupping them.

Soft. She is so soft and squeezable. I want to touch every inch of her. To memorize every spot that arouses her. I lick and suck, tasting her, teasing her. My hands roam over her body. She is so sweet, so responsive, and everything the manuals claimed she would be. My cock is throbbing and my *seela* are reaching for her as I slowly make my way up her body, settling my knees between her thighs and spreading her legs wide. Responding to my desires, the Bride Trainer retracts, turning into a belt around her curvy hips, revealing her to me fully.

Her dark pink pussy gleams with wetness, displaying her arousal, and I want to crow with triumph. Finally. Everything I ever wanted, everything I have worked for all these long tsencycles, is here as my reward.

My sweet Tribute. My Marta.

* * *

MARTA

Arkdhem is absolutely wicked with his tongue and hands, and if I didn't believe in aliens, the only other explanation my brain might be able to come up with is that I've died and gone to heaven. But I do believe in aliens, and right now this one is doing absolutely sinful things to my body. He's exploring every inch of me, touching me, tasting me, and by the time he's spreading my thighs and lining up his cock with my pussy, the tiny tentacles—his *seela*—don't seem like such a big deal. Weird alien peen is kind of to be expected, anyway.

The longest one at the top taps against my clit as he begins to push inside me and I gasp at the sensation, my hands fisting in the sheets. Kneeling between my legs, he looks down and watches his cock as it presses into me, opening me up, and I can't reach him at all. My hands clench around the sheets beneath me, needing something to grip as hot pleasure rushes along my veins. I whimper, my head thrashing back and forth as the strangely shaped tip stretches me open in a completely different way than a human cock would.

I can actually feel it moving inside me, the sides gently flapping and stroking against the walls of my pussy. Arkdhem groans, shuddering, and pushes deeper. The bumps and ridges along his cock are the most delicious friction as he starts moving, thrusting a little deeper with each stroke, filling me a little more. His cock seems to swell inside me. He rocks his hips slightly and lights burst behind my eyes, an odd keening noise escaping from my lips.

I feel so full, so hot. My body is on fire for him.

Then the little suckers fasten onto my labia and inner thighs, tightening and pulling me closer until Arkdhem and I are joined by multiple tentacles. The sensation is intensely pleasurable and I cry out, gasping in shock. They're like nothing I've ever felt before.

Arkdhem reverses his glide, pulling out so only the wedge head of his cock rests in my pussy. The little tentacles pop off and wave like sea anemones in the ocean current, as if desperate to reattach themselves. Arkdhem slides back and sheathes himself fully inside me. Everything inside me clenches. My orgasm blooms slowly, a satisfying warmth in my belly.

Yes. This is what I need.

"More… fuck me, Arkdhem… I need more…"

Arkdhem moves in a sensual rhythm, his cock curving deep inside me, slowly picking up his pace. Each time he bottoms out, the wavy ridge of the biggest *seela* catches the edge of my clit, tickling it. I rock to greet it eagerly, rubbing myself against his body and the long tentacle. As if sensing my desire, it somehow latches on to my clit, producing a sucking sensation, as if a tiny mouth has begun suckling my most sensitive organ.

White hot ecstasy blasts through me so hard and fast that my eyes roll back into my head and I scream as my entire body tenses. I feel like I'm about to levitate, the intense pleasure rocking through me, leaving me panting.

The suckling sensation immediately stops and my watery muscles go lax, leaving me whimpering.

Arkdhem has stilled, concern on his face. "Marta? Are you all right?"

"Yes. Oh, god, don't stop. Please don't stop." It doesn't matter that I just had a massive orgasm, my body wants more of him. Craves more. The burning sensation hasn't quite stopped, like an itch that needs to be scratched, and I need him to keep fucking me. I need to feel him come in me.

Is this something the priming has done to me? Because I've never felt like this before. Or maybe it's the 'bond' Frllil talked about, that I didn't put a lot of stock in. Now I wish I'd paid a bit more attention, but I figured he'd been talking about an emotional bond. Not a physical one.

Taking me at my word, Arkdhem starts to thrust again. Tears of pure happiness leak down my cheeks as a wave of ecstasy makes my pussy clench. Now that he's reassured I'm well, it's like a dam has broken, and he's fucking me harder and harder into the mattress. The *seela* reattaches itself to my clit and starts suckling and I scream and writhe in glorious, filthy rapture.

I'm coming and coming again, the golden ripples of pleasure rolling, cresting, breaking over me. I've barely come up for air when another climax pulls me under. I scream. I sob. I writhe in abject pleasure as my alien lover fucks me senseless. Arkdhem groans, gripping my bottom and rocking with greater urgency. The tentacles pop on and off depending on his proximity, doing their best to seal us together.

Arkdhem's powerful body moves over me. His cock probes deeper with each thrust. I wrap my legs around his hips, dig my fingernails into his golden skin to pull him closer, and hang on for the ride. Sweat slicks my body. Arkdhem's jaw is tensed and his eyes glitter as he palms my ass and hitches me closer. The broad head of his cock bumps a spot deep inside me and I explode again with a shout. My insides quake. Only his body pressing me into the bed holds me together.

"Yes…" The huge Tsenturion slides almost all the way out and slams back inside, bumping the spot again. I can barely hear him over my own gasping cries. "Come for me again, my sweet Tribute. My heart."

* * *

Arkdhem

MY TRIBUTE'S inner muscles pulse against my cock as I slide in deep. Her climax is almost continuous now. Her knees grip me. My *seela* suction tight to her smooth skin, hard enough to leave red marks. I want to mark her. To paint my name on her skin with my cum and leave it there for her to wear. When the time came to wipe it off, I'd immediately mark her again.

I've never had such possessive thoughts, but now that I've had them, they won't stop coming.

If Marta ever has to leave the room, I want her swathed in robes with a sign hanging from a chain around her neck reading 'Arkdhem's Tribute.' Or maybe I'll just keep her in my room forever, tied up and waiting for me, the ship systems monitoring her vital signs so I can return to her side at a moment's notice. Or keep her caged near the bed, just outside of my work zone so I can keep an eye on her.

Yes, that's preferable. We never have to leave the room again.

I want to bury myself inside her and stay here, always.

And with that thought, I come deep inside my tribute for the very first time. She cries out as my seed floods her, her body arching, and I lean forward, pressing my forehead against hers. She reaches up and wraps her arms around me, her lips meeting mine in a desperate kiss.

My cock pulses inside her as I delve my tongue into her mouth, our bodies pressed so tightly together, it feels as though we are one.

And, in some way, we are. Our nanotech is now fully bonded. I can feel her body around me, against me, feel her heart beating rapidly in her chest against mine. She is now my everything, and I vow we will never be separated again.

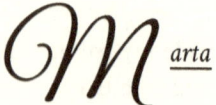 *arta*

MY EYES ARE HALF-CLOSED and I'm lying on the bed, blissed out on pleasure. Arkdhem glides out of me slowly and I shudder with aftershocks. My pussy feels empty without him, but it also feels sore as hell. He gave me more orgasms than I could count, and I'm torn between wanting more, and wanting to sleep for a week.

Arkdhem leans over me, his large form casting a shadow over my face. My eyes are a little unfocused. I blink. I may have fallen asleep for a moment, overcome with the after-glow. And now, long fingers are stroking my cheeks, smoothing my eyebrows.

Arkdhem traces down my nose and his thumb rubs my lips. I smile so he knows I'm awake but he doesn't stop exploring my skin with long, soothing strokes. His fingers follow the curve of my neck and shoulder, then dip down between my breasts.

He's exploring me, but without the urgency he had before. It feels both odd and nice, and as soon as I can get up the energy, I want to return the favor.

He touches one nipple and toys with the rising flesh. It crinkles at his touch and that seems to fascinate him. I shudder a little at the newly rising pleasure trickling through me. Arkdhem circles a finger around the flat brown areola before returning to my nipple, and I moan. He runs his knuckles under my breast and caresses every inch of my flesh. It's a long while before he moves on, and even though I've been thoroughly sexed up, my body's already stirring again.

Though, I guess it's not that surprising. I spent days being primed. It's probably going to take a full-on sex marathon to sate me.

His fingers drift lower down, poking and exploring my belly button. Now my hips are shifting as he moves lower yet. I want to jump him again.

"Have you ever seen a human woman before?" I ask. My voice is husky, strained. Maybe I was screaming a little loudly, there at the end.

His hands still but he doesn't take them away. "I have."

Oh, right, duh. He met the other Tributes. But did he see them naked? Did they let him touch him like this?

A shot of jealousy makes me push up to my elbows and ask, "Like this?"

"No, my heart. Never like this." He's almost smiling, as if he knows I'm jealous and he likes it. His answer reassures me and I settle back onto the bed. He resumes stroking down my sides. I want to arch against him like a cat. Who knew that I like to be petted? "I have seen other Tributes, yes. But none naked." His voice deepens. "And none so lovely as you."

I'm stretching and preening like a pampered pet, and now I want to purr.

His fingers have found the soft skin of my inner thighs. He laves my legs with long strokes. I stretch my thighs wide, letting my labia open like a flower. Here's hoping he'll take the hint and touch me where I'm aching. But nope, he ignores my throbbing sex. He spends a minute running his fingers over my upper thighs and contrasting that with the silky skin in between, as if fascinated by the difference. Then he grips my calves. His massaging fingers release all the tension in my body. He grasps my foot, and his thumbs run up my arch. He discovers how ticklish I am, and also the groaning noises I make when he rubs the tension out of a particular spot. I feel totally pampered and boneless, and also incredibly turned on.

But instead taking advantage of this, he rises off the bed. *Meu deus*, that is a beautiful body. Tall, broad shouldered, golden with all sorts of muscles that a human man doesn't even have. All in the glittering gold of his skin. The weird cock that is already erect again, despite the fact that he pulled away.

"Are you hungry, my Tribute?"

Sure I am… for him. My stomach gives a little grumble.

Right. Sex burns calories. And epic sex burns a lot more. And that was epic, even if it was vanilla. Although, the tentacles were an unexpected bonus.

"A little," I admit, even though I'm pretty sure it's going to delay my turn for sexploration. Food is fuel, after all, and I don't want to pass out from hunger before I get the chance to do so from pleasure.

He nods absently and starts walking away, still gazing at my prone form lounging on the bed as if he can't tear his eyes away. He goes to the wall and says something. I'm too distracted by his tight, gold, naked buns to see what's happening, and the next thing I know, he's carrying a tray full of dishes back to the bed. Whatever's on the tray smells amazing even if the food looks strange. From here, it looks like lots of bright blue and purple foods—a clash of colors I've never seen in food before. One dish holds mounds of what looks like ice cream but it smells meaty. My mouth waters.

Arkdhem sets the tray on the bed. "The replicator can make food from your planet, but I thought you could try some of my favorites as well. At least one of the other Tributes likes each of them, so I know they are compatible with humans."

"You thought right," I say, because my favorite thing to do in a new country is go to an outdoor market or grocery store and be dazzled by the unfamiliar foods and packaging. I'm also touched by his thoughtfulness that he's offering foods he knows that one other human likes. I'll probably try everything eventually, because that's how I am, but starting with things I'll hopefully enjoy sounds good.

My stomach is asking for food, *now*, so I reach for what looks familiar—a plate of square brown cookies in the corner. British type tea biscuits. I could eat the whole plate, and maybe I will. I just burned a thousand calories, right?

Before my fingers touch the biscuits, Arkdhem gently catches my wrist and guides my hand away. He holds the first bite of something to my mouth: a purple fruit that has a knobby surface.

I close my eyes as I part my lips, feeling the brush of his fingers against them as he puts the piece in my mouth. The purple fruit has a knobby surface and citrusy flavor like an orange, and the texture of avocado. It's surprisingly good.

"So these are your quarters?" I ask after I swallow. If he's not sexing me up, I want to know more about where I am. I am a question machine, and if he's going to be my mate, he's going to have to get used to that.

"Yes." He offers up another bite to eat and I give up trying to figure out why something that looks like ice cream smells meaty. I close my eyes again and just let the flavors burst on my tongue. It tastes like steak but the texture is more pasty, kind of like a paté.

"So, you've never had a Tribute?" I know the answer, having reviewed the files, but I want him to keep talking. I want to know more about him, specifically, and I'm hoping to get more than a one-word answer. He's going to need to get used to being peppered with questions and giving more satisfactory answers. I require it of the people close to me. It's probably why my boyfriends didn't last very long—that and my work schedule, and general lack of interest in keeping a relationship.

"No." He takes a moment to stroke my lips, even though I'm not a messy eater and I don't think I've spilled anything. The gesture feels incredibly intimate and he stares into my eyes, making it even more so. "You are my first. My only."

My stomach is getting full. I don't even know what I've eaten. I keep expecting him to explain what these foods are but he seems to be preoccupied with just watching me. He hasn't even eaten, himself. When he's picking up another bite, I snatch a tea biscuit and offer it to his mouth. "You must be hungry."

He smiles a little and lets me feed him. His features are mostly humanoid. I can't get over the strange golden skin. I end up stroking his face and now I understand why he took so long to explore me. His skin is silky smooth to my touch, warm, and the more I touch him, the more I want to.

"Where is your suit?" I ask, tracing the edge of his jaw. Before my question is over, his armor is rising from his skin, forming right under my fingertips into the lower half of a helmet. Almost like a medieval knight's armor, but with the ability to shape itself.

"This is the suit," he says. "It responds to my mental commands."

I run my hands down his shoulders. His armor is still rising, growing wicked-looking spines that curve from his back. I would hate to fight someone wearing this. I guess that's the point. My not-panties aren't nearly as cool, although it's nice to know they can be a belt instead of underwear.

Arkdhem is a warrior. From what I've read, the Tsenturions are a military culture. I filed that away as useful information and intellectually, I understood, but it's another thing to lie in bed with my new lover and see it first hand. It reminds me of the great loss he and his people have endured and my stomach twists with sympathy for them. I can't even imagine the kind of rage and grief he's felt... and yet here he is with me, seeming perfectly happy.

It places an unexpected burden on my shoulders. The idea of being a Tribute, a female to fuck, was easy in some ways. Emotional stuff... not so much. I'm not a touchy-feely person, at all. I didn't expect to feel emotions for him, especially not so soon after meeting him, but it's hard not to when I think about what he endured.

So I do what I do best: I distract myself and keep touching him, focusing on the armor and his skin, and how the two are both the same and different. On a scientific level, it's fascinating.

Arkdhem seems content to let me explore him as he explored me earlier, so I don't stop.

"My skin and my suit are bonded. The nanites make it one and the same."

"Incredible." So are all these epic muscles of his chest and shoulders and arms. He's leaner than some of the images of the Tsenturions I've seen, but just as built. He has the tight muscles of a marathon runner, or a mountain climber.

And he's mine, all mine.

I spread my hands over his pectoral muscles—or what would be called his pectoral muscles if he were a human man. If I could, I would purr with satisfaction. Without thinking, I move into his lap so I'm on my knees straddling him, my thighs spread wide. I'm definitely not having any issues with my emotions now—I've only got one emotion going on, and it's desire. My core touches his muscled midriff. His large hands come to support my back and the armor flashes gold before melting into his skin as if it was never there at all.

"So… you've never shared your quarters with anyone?" I venture, curious, as I run my hands over his newly smoothed shoulders. Frllil's files were full of information, but they didn't contain anything. Humans are the first species found that are genetically compatible with Tsenturions, supposedly, but there was no indication of whether or not they've ever found another sexually compatible species.

"Not since becoming an officer. I've been here alone." There's a sadness in his eyes that tugs at me, reaching out to those messy emotions I'm trying to ignore. I should move on from the topic, but I'm too surprised to change the subject.

"All this time? You've never… been with anyone?" He's had duties and held a military office. But if what he's telling me is right, he hasn't had sex for a thousand years. And he still took the time to go down on me before sexing me up. Impressive.

"Yes," he replies. "I've waited for you, my Marta."

Holy shit, not only did I fuck an alien, I popped his cherry! Also—*holy crap*! If he was that good at sex the first time, I can only imagine what he'll be like when he's had some practice. Though, as he said, he did have the 'manuals', aka the sex books. Back on Earth, women wish men would read romance and take some notes. Here, I have an alien who has been using them as instruction manuals, and I am not complaining.

I rock a little bit against him. Ooh, that feels nice. I can rub my clit right against the edges of his muscles.

His cheeks widen with his smile. He knows what I'm doing but he seems willing to allow it. His hands reaffirm their grip on my ass as he dips his head close. "You were worth the wait."

We're chest to chest, sitting as intimately as a couple can. I've just met him, but this feels right. My desire ramps up even as I continue to question him. "So you spent all those years on duty or here, no breaks?"

"It was easier to lose myself in work than do anything else. For all of us. I was hardly the only one."

Right, the destruction of his people. I stop rocking against him. "I'm sorry for your loss."

"Thank you," he says. "It was a long time ago." The grief flickering in his eyes belies his statement. He reminds me of some of the soldiers I met back on Earth, those who would joke about their experiences with hollow eyes and voices. Then he blinks, and the emotion is gone, hidden away, the same way as the veterans I'd met. His hands glide up my back, still exploring. He adds, in a wondering tone, as if he can't believe his luck, "For so long, we've had nothing but vengeance, justice, to drive us, but then Frllil told us he'd found a compatible species. Now we have hope again, a future we can build towards. And now I have you."

The way he looks at me... as if I'm some kind of reward that's worth having been alone for so long. My heart aches.

"So you really have been around for a thousand years?" The mind boggles. I can't imagine. I'm in my thirties and I feel old beyond my years sometimes, with everything I've done and seen, but that's nothing compared to him.

"Oh yes, the nanites remove any sign of aging. And now you will live as long as I do."

"Seems like a long time." I frown. I've forgotten to keep rubbing against him. Now I want to research... But I also want more sex. Decisions, decisions. But my first instinct has always been to follow the story. "What—"

"Patience, my heart," Arkdhem interrupts me, smiling. The heat in his eyes tells me exactly what he is thinking, and I can feel his *seela* beginning to writhe against my thighs again. It's an odd sensation, but arousing as well, especially because I know exactly how they feel now. "There is plenty of time for questions. But right now, I have another pressing need."

One of his hands comes between us and his fingers strum my lower folds, seeking out my clit. I whimper a little, squirming on top of him.

"But... I want to know..." My voice is a little bit breathless. Conflicted. Because I don't know what I want more—him, or answers.

Smack!

His palm lightly cracks on my right buttock. I straighten and stiffen, then melt. The heat from the sting is delicious. Nothing like a little bit of punishment to get my head in the right space for intimacy. Amazing that this alien light years away from my home planet gets that better than any guy I've ever dated.

My hips tilt forward again so I can rub myself against him exactly how I want. He smacks his left hand against my left buttock.

Yes! Spank me, golden alien daddy!

He grips the back of my neck, arching me backwards. I quiver in his hold. He's totally in control, and my body revels in it. Being dominated like this has always been the only way to get my brain to turn off during sex. "There will be time for you to learn all you wish to know. For now, I am going to fuck you again. The manuals say that to complete your claiming in the manner of your people, I must earn your submission."

Oh, well, damn. That sounds hot. And fascinating. Also possibly painful. All the filthy hot books I read start running through my head, with all the sinfully sexy scenes. I might be in trouble here, but my nipples are already perked up and I'm wet all over again, and not just from his seed.

He keeps spanking me lightly, his left hand still gripping my hair and tugging my head back so my face is turned upwards. He seems to be studying all my expressions, the way I jolt when his hand smacks down particularly hard, the way I quiver when his fingers massage my bottom.

His fingers explore the crack of my ass, and I stiffen. I've never done anal play with another guy, though I've read about it and I've wanted to. I've done some explorations on my own, but they were more uncomfortable than anything else. Definitely nothing like how my books made it sound. But Arkdhem's long index finger is like magic, sliding into my ass, slick and hard, and making me feel so hot and full. The sensation is both strange and good. I shudder, letting my head fall back as I moan.

He goes back to smacking my ass again. A low burn develops in my sit-spots. The heat warms my whole core, and my hips rock faster.

I'm close to orgasm when he tugs my hair, turning me and pulling me over his lap. I land on my belly over his hard thighs, with my bottom pointing upward and my face almost to the bed.

Once I'm in position, he splays a hand between my shoulder blades, keeping me down. His other hand is free to toy with my upturned buttocks and the seam beneath my cheeks. I wriggle, trying to get my clit the stimulation it needs so I can come, and he smacks my bottom harder.

"Be still, my sweet Tribute," he orders, and my belly clenches at the commanding tone.

He explores my lower lips. Finding the wetness of my pussy, he chuckles to himself. He can tell that I'm loving this.

I can't keep my hips from twitching as his fingers dance over my folds. He's got me pinned, and damn if I don't find that hot. I try to get my hands free and he catches them too, pinning my wrists in the small of my back.

And then his finger goes back to probing my bottom. He circles my bottom hole and I tighten my buttocks automatically to keep him out. Another chuckle above my head, and he goes back to spanking me in an even pattern. Left, right, left, right. A few slaps to my upper thighs, and the lower curve of my bottom. Lightly at first, awakening warmth in my cheeks. Once I've relaxed, he increases the intensity. The stinging slaps spark more heat in my rear, but with the endorphins washing through me, I'm floating. I'm so high, I barely notice when he stops.

He shifts me off his lap and onto a pillow. I'm still belly down, with my throbbing bottom propped high. Perfect for spanking—or doggy style.

And, yep, after a few more playful smacks to my heated flesh, he's parting my legs and gliding into me from behind. My sex is sopping, and yields to his hard girth. There's a delicious stretch and then he's bottomed out in my pussy, his taut groin pressed against my burning buttocks. I groan into the rumpled bedding.

He winds his fingers into my hair again and tugs my head back. To relieve the pressure, my back arches, and I push my chest off the bed. He reaches a hand around to my front and delves between my legs to find my clit.

"Come for me, my Tribute." His clever fingers catch the

sweet spot to the left of my clit. My climax muscles are already quivering.

I'm going to be so sore tomorrow.

But I don't care.

I come hard, screaming his name.

CHAPTER 5

*A*rkdhem

          Having a Tribute is so much more than I imagined.

For so long, jealousy and envy consumed me when I looked at Dawn and Pareena, especially Pareena. I did not think that Bogden was worthy of her. I hated him for receiving a Tribute before me. But now, I understand.

Pareena was never meant to be mine, because the universe was bringing Marta to me. I had become impatient, thinking any Tribute would do, but now I know, no one but Marta would complete me.

Lying on my side, I lean on my elbow, looking down at her and memorizing every feature on her beautiful face. Her tanned skin, a beautiful bronze color somewhere between Dawn and Pareena's shades, the slope of her nose, the long, black eyelashes that brush against her cheeks. She sighs softly in her sleep and turns her face towards me. After I claimed her several more times and thoroughly pleasured her, we ate another round of food supplied by the replicator and she fell asleep almost immediately afterwards, satisfied in every way.

I reach out to run my fingers through her hair. It is curlier than either Pareena or Dawn's and multi-hued, with both darker undertones and lighter strands that almost match her skin, as if she combined both of their hair colors. I am fascinated. Human females come in such a wide variety of shapes and colors. Tsenturions are all gold, without any of the differences, with similar body types.

My comm unit chimes, and I growl under my breath at the interruption. *Drakk.* I do not need to answer to know why they are calling. We are a single ship, and I need to be on the bridge for my shift. I did not want to ask my fellow warriors to take over my duties so that I can indulge myself with my Tribute, now I am wishing I had.

But duty calls.

I push to my feet as Marta moves beside me, suddenly stirring now that I am getting up, and blinking sleepily at me.

"Where are you going?"

"I have a shift on the bridge. I will be back. Stay here. Rest." I lean down and press my lips to her forehead. My armor slides over my body, covering me. I send a signal to the nanotech, and her Bride Trainer grows from her belt to cover her again.

"But—"

I give her a stern look.

"You will need rest. I will have food sent to you. When I return, I will take you on a tour of the ship."

Turning on my heel, I leave the room quickly. Not because I want to, but because it is so hard to, and the more I look at her and her adorable pout, the less I want to leave. My body aches to return to her the moment I begin walking down the hall, despite being physically sated. It is as though I cannot get enough of her.

Is this how it always was between mates? I do not know. I do not remember. It has been so long since we lost the rest of our people, and I was not ready for a mate when the last festival was held. Perhaps I should ask someone… but does it really matter?

That is the past. Marta is my present, and my future.

* * *

MARTA

As the door slides shut behind Arkdhem, I groan. There is no way I'm staying here like a good little girl and waiting for him to come show me around. I can make my own way around, thank you very much. And I am way too curious to stay cramped up in here all day, not knowing when he'll be back. There's nothing to do in here.

Arkdhem is happy to have a Tribute and to get laid—can't blame him there—but either he clearly knows nothing about humans, or the previous two Tributes were utterly lacking in curiosity.

I groan as I roll over and get to my feet.

I'm sore in places I've never been sore before. That alien cock hit all sorts of spots that no man ever touched, and the *seela*… Looking down, I giggle as I see all the red hickey spots he left on my thighs, and I know there are more under the panties. Tentacle hickeys. They look ridiculous, and yet I like seeing them too. Which strikes me as a little odd.

Back on Earth, I never let a man mark me. But then, human men didn't have tentacle pubes to help pleasure me. And it always felt like men wanted to leave hickeys to mark me as a possession. No one is going to see these.

I make a face at the panties. Those, I could have done without. But they're not as bad now that I've gotten my big O

44

several times over. Actually, my vagina could probably use some armor right now, to help protect it.

First things first. I inspect the room. There's nowhere to keep clothes—which makes sense when I remember that Arkdhem literally wears his in his skin. There's the pile of books, of course, but nothing else I can see for entertainment. The bathroom is nice, with a large tub and shower area.

But there's nothing that makes me want to stay in here longer than I have to. Looking around, I see there are no clothes for me either—other than the robe I arrived in, which Arkdhem had tossed on the floor. The ceremonial gown might not be much, but it's what I have. I've gone undercover wearing less in the past. Shrugging it back on, I head for the door. Unlike for Arkdhem, it doesn't immediately slide open when I approach.

"Open." The door remains firmly shut.

No wonder Arkdhem thought he could leave me cooped up in here. I scowl. Kick the door. Hmph.

A memory stirs in my consciousness. When I was with Frllil, on one of the days I was exploring, I followed him into a room that was kind of like a library, with a lot of shelves, and he either didn't realize or forgot, and accidentally locked me in there. Once he realized what had happened, he taught me the override command, which was supposed to be used in such situations. He'd said it worked in almost all Jabol locations.

This was a Tsenturion ship, but an awful lot of it looked exactly like Frllil's setup so maybe they used the same technology...

"Bllilligillar." The door swooshes open. "Ha!" I pump my fist in the air. That's Marta: 1, Bossy Alien: 0.

Stepping out into the hall, I look around. It's empty, no sign of other Tsenturion warriors anywhere around. Lots of grey walls. No decoration. But it is a military ship, so that's not exactly surprising. It's also not particularly interesting.

Are you sure you want to do this? The cautious side of my brain rears its head at the most inopportune times. *Arkdhem is not going to be happy, and you know what happens in those books you read when the alien isn't happy.*

Oooh, spankings. I've always wanted to be spanked. And the little slaps he gave me during the last round of hide-the-weird-alien-peen sparked my curiosity. Of course, it'll probably hurt too. But, even though I haven't known him very long, I can't imagine Arkdhem actually harming me.

Is it weird to trust an alien I've never seen until he became my mate? Absolutely. Yet, I can't shake the conviction that I'm safe with him. Maybe it's a side effect of the nanotech. Frllil did say there would be some.

Wandering down the corridor, I don't bother trying any of the doors. I'm assuming that the Tsenturions don't all bunk in the same hall, which means these should all be bedrooms. I don't want to disturb anyone at rest, and I definitely don't want to be stopped to answer questions.

When I get to the first crossroads, I do a quick eeny-meeny-minie-moe, and end up taking a right hand turn. This corridor looks exactly the same as the previous corridor. I wonder if I'm still walking past bedrooms.

About halfway down the hall, I come to a grinding halt as the right hand side of the corridor opens up into a kind of sitting area. But it's not just any sitting area. There are a few couches and benches, yes, but the main point of it is the huge window that looks out into space.

I gasp, slowly walking towards the big, open blackness. Seeing how far it goes outside the window is giving me a weird kind of vertigo, but it's like I'm hypnotized by the sight. I can't look away, and I need to get closer.

A foot away from the glass, I come to a halt and reach out

a shaking hand. Being able to see my reflection is the only reason it doesn't look like I'm reaching out into the blackness of space itself. I can see stars off in the distance, so far away, and I suddenly feel very, very small and insignificant.

But it's so beautiful.

* * *

Arkdhem

Everything is going smoothly for the trip back to the fleet. Too smoothly.

I know eventually I will have to face the High Commander again, and that he will not be happy. While I remain ready to face whatever repercussions my actions have wrought against me, I am aware of every passing microcycle of our return trip, because each microcycle brings me closer to the end of this easy bonding time with Marta.

When the return trip ends, I will be subject to disciplinary measures, and I do not know how much time any punishment will allow me to have with my Tribute.

I almost wish for some kind of interruption, some sort of small delay, to give me more uninterrupted time with her.

Sensing my distraction, Argan turns to me.

"Commander, if you like, I can maintain the course and alert you only if an issue arises."

Having already not done my duty once—leaving the fleet to retrieve my Tribute rather than following through with the orders the High Commander gave me—I am loath to leave my command post but... the trip is going smoothly. And I do not want to waste one precious microcycle with Marta.

Finally I nod, albeit a bit reluctantly. "Thank you, Argan."

"Of course." He grins, fist to his chest in salute. "We all

need to make accommodations for the reception of a new Tribute."

That is true. I remember that the High Commander himself left Bogdan and me in charge of the fleet after Dawn joined us. Feeling a little better, I salute Argan back, and leave the bridge.

My feet move much faster returning to my quarters than they did leaving, my heart lightening with every step I take. 'Eager' does not begin to describe how I feel. I want nothing more than to spend all of my time with Marta, until our inevitable return to the fleet.

As soon as I reach the door, it registers my nanotech, and slides open to admit me.

"I am back!" I stride into the room with a wide grin on my face. But there is no answer. And there is no Marta sprawled out on the bed where I left her. My heart begins to pound rapidly. The door to the bathing room is open, and she is not there either. I rush through the room anyway, as if there is somewhere she could be hiding from me, and then back out into the hall, looking back and forth frantically.

Where the drakk is she?

* * *

Marta

"Marta!" My name is roared so loudly that, even far down the hall, I jump and whirl around.

I'm not sure what's behind the door that I'm currently trying to get into, but the fact that it's locked and also resists the override command that Frllil taught me has my curiosity burning. I can hear the upset in Arkdhem's voice, though, as he yells my name again.

My butt is already tingling, as if in either anticipation or warning, because yup, my big sexy has discovered my absence, and he's pissed.

"I'm here!" I yell back, hoping that maybe if I act like everything is fine, I'll mend some of the damage. Also, I know from my books that trying to hide or escape the consequences will probably result in a heavier punishment than facing up to it.

"Marta?" Arkdhem rounds the corner and sees me standing at the end of the hall. His suit is flashing red and yellow, and the bright colors are only partially soothed when he lays eyes on me. The yellow dwindles, leaving mostly red. "What are you doing outside the armory?"

"Is that what this is?" Damn. Now I really wish I'd been able to get in. Not that I think I would need a weapon to protect myself from Arkdhem, but I also don't like the idea of being completely defenseless… plus, I bet they have some cool stuff in there.

Arkdhem comes to a halt in front of me, crossing his arms over his chest. I don't need the brightly flashing red armor to tell me that he is one pissed-off mate—I can see it all over his face. Shit. Putting my hands behind me, I bat my eyelashes innocently as he stares down at me.

I'm not scared, exactly, but I'm starting to think that maybe the impetuous decision to wander about the ship on my own wasn't that smart. To be fair, I'd expected him to be gone a *lot* longer. And I hadn't actually agreed to his command that I stay put.

"How did you get out of the room?" His voice is low and tight, like he's holding back from yelling at me again through sheer willpower.

"I walked through the door." It's the truth. I've been in court enough to know never to give more information than is asked for. Keep it simple, honest, and—above all—don't volunteer anything.

Arkdhem narrows his eyes at me. "The door was locked."

"Was it? Then how did I get out?" I bat my eyelashes again. Yeah, it's cliché, but hey, it worked more than once on Earth, so why not now? Might as well try. I arch my back, pushing my breasts up as well. His gaze drops to them and he silently stares at my boobs for a long moment.

Hooray for boobies! Weapons of mass distraction all over the universe.

Unfortunately, it doesn't take very long for him to remember that he's mad, though at least he does seem a little less mad than he was a second ago.

He scowls at me and holds up his arm. A little video appears above his wrist and it takes me a moment to realize that it's basically a door cam, showing me coming up to the door. Dammit.

"Bllilligillar." My voice sounds odd and tinny, but it's clear. "Ha!" Video me pumps my fist in the air. I sigh. I just had to celebrate, didn't I?

"Sorry?" I say, wrinkling my nose and trying to look as sweet and innocent as possible.

It doesn't work.

Arkdhem literally tosses me over his shoulder like I weigh nothing and swings around, heading down the hall, carrying me like a sack of potatoes.

"Hey! Arkdhem! I really am sorry!"

Smack!

The swat to my ass is nothing like the playful ones he gave me before, and I gasp at the painful sting.

"You certainly will be," he says darkly. My sweet cinnamon roll has a stern side, and I've awoken the beast.

"I already am! I promise, I won't do it again." I'm babbling. I never babble. On the other hand, I've never been tossed over someone's shoulder and spanked before either.

* * *

Arkdhem

My Marta is a strong-willed female, I can tell. I like her that way, but certain orders are for her safety. While I trust my fellow warriors with my life, it's a whole other thing to trust them with my mate. I do not want to break her will, at all, but she does need to bend, at least until she learns our customs and rules. I shake my head at all the trouble she could have gotten into on her own.

She gasps and wriggles on my shoulder as the Bride Trainer pushes relentlessly into her bottom hole and begins to pulse. The manual put particular emphasis on how important that hole is to putting a female into the proper submissive mindset. I had not been particularly interested in it, because it is not necessary for breeding, but now I realize ignoring it may have been a mistake—one I will not make again.

"Arkdhem, please!"

Already I can tell it is working. She sounds much less defiant and sassy than she did when I first confronted her. And when she lied to me.

The door to our chambers slides open again and I carry my squirming mate inside and over to the bed. Putting her on her feet, I quickly strip her dress back off while she stares up at me pleadingly.

She might protest, but I can feel her arousal through the beginnings of our bond. The hard buds of her nipples are standing at attention again, begging to be pinched and sucked. Despite my anger and disappointment, my cock surges to life, my *seela* begin to writhe. I am not sure there is anything she can do that will quench my desire for her.

That will not save her from a deserved punishment. The manuals were very clear, and I witnessed how well the tactics worked with Dawn and Pareena; it is best to start as I mean to go on. That means I cannot give her leniency for a first offense, doing so would only encourage her to offend again.

"Turn around and bend over." I cross my arms over my chest, my gaze stern. My armor is no longer flashing red, but the neutral black still flickers with it.

Marta's mouth opens and closes, as if she was about to protest and then thought the better of it. Good. Ducking her head, she turns around and bends over the bed. The sight of her obedience, as well as her beautiful bottom pointing at me, sets my pulse racing. She is perfection.

"Good girl." I send an order to her nanotech and the Bride Trainer recedes into her belt, except for a thin line that travels down the crease of her bottom and into it, where her small hole is stretched around its insertion. "Now you will stay there and think about what you've done wrong while I make a call."

It is only the work of a few moments to contact the bridge and tell them to update the overrides. It is something we probably should have done anyway, now that we know the Jabol are possible enemies. We are in ships they provided for us, and we have never changed the override commands, because we trusted them.

I make a mental note to tell Gavrill to change the rest of the fleet's as well.

Then I turn my attention back to Marta, studying her in silence from behind. My mate is beginning to squirm again.

CHAPTER 6

@M *arta*
Waiting is awful.

Some things, I am very patient about. Waiting for the perfect lead to follow. Tracking a tiny thread of information. Letting silence hang in the air while I wait for someone to confess their secrets to me.

But waiting for a spanking? Nope. I just want to get it started. Waiting for it to happen is awful. And I know that's exactly why he's making me wait. The big jerk. Some cinnamon roll he's turning out to be.

And yet, this bossy side of his is turning me on. Even without the panties humming against my pussy, I know I'd be squirming. It makes no sense. I've never liked being bossed around. Then again, I've never had a guy try to do it in the bedroom. They always assumed that because I was so independent outside of it, I wouldn't want to be submissive inside of it, and I had felt too ashamed to ask.

It really is like one of my books come to life, and my pussy is aching. Even the thick probe that's filled my ass is turning me on. I've never done anything anal before, and it hurts and feels good all at the same time—and he's not wrong about it making me feel more submissive too. It's hard to feel large and in charge with something rammed up my butt.

It's been quiet back there for a minute.

Is he looking at me?

Is he ignoring me?

I peek over my shoulder, and then whip my head back around.

He was totally looking at me.

My pussy gets wetter. Hotter.

Knowing that he's staring at me from behind, waiting for him to come spank me... Yes, the waiting is awful but it's also hot as hell.

The room is so quiet that I can hear him as he moves up behind me, placing his hand on the cheek of my ass. My muscles clench around the nanotech plug, making the stretched entrance ache.

"Do you understand why you're being punished, my heart?" His voice is firm, but gentle, his hand caressing the spot where I know he's going to spank me first. My heart races, my pulse pounding so loud, I can actually hear it.

"Because I left the room after you told me not to." I mean to sound defiant, but somehow my voice comes out small.

"And because you lied to me about it."

Oh. Right.

His hand lifts and comes crashing down on my ass. This is no playful swat. It stings and burns and I shriek, jerking upright. I don't make it very far before there's a hand between my shoulder blades, shoving me back down into place.

My pussy quivers.

I am so fucked.

* * *

Arkdhem

The thick fall of Marta's dark brown hair spills over her shoulder. Her bare bottom is a work of art. The Bride Trainer frames her rear cheeks, flowing over her hips like a harness that holds the plug in her bottom. Lower down, the chastity belt-like piece has opened to give me access to her plump lower lips. The dark curls framing her pouting labia are already slick, and the honeyed scent of her arousal fills the air.

I thoroughly researched the manuals in preparation to receive my Tribute, but the reality is better. I send a command to the Bride Trainer to widen the plug inside her, and a little gasp greets me as it stretches her from the inside out.

I rub her upturned bottom, stroking the silky skin almost reverently. Her plump curves make me ache to claim her. The only thing better will be the sight of her punished bottom glowing red.

I set my left hand in the small of her back to steady her. My first slap makes her gasp. I admire the slight jiggle, and the faint mark of my handprint.

This will be a much harder spanking than the one earlier. She enjoyed that spanking. She will not enjoy this one—at least, not during her punishment. I may allow her to come once she has been thoroughly subjugated. While I enjoy my Marta's fiery intelligence and curious spirit, when it counts, I mean for her to give me her submission and her surrender. With training, she will be the perfect Tribute.

I smack her left cheek and then her right. I divide her bottom into several quadrants and make sure I pepper each evenly. Her upper thighs and sit-spots get their own share of attention, and soon her entire backside is painted pink. She's wriggling and moaning. My cock is painfully hard.

I flip her onto her back, and her eyes widen in surprise. As pleasant as it is to watch her bottom turn bright pink, then maroon, I wish to see her face. I hold up her legs and continue punishing her. Each swat makes her jolt, causing her breasts to bounce. It gives me an idea.

I give another command to the Bride Trainer. It streams up her front to circle her breasts, framing them.

It's an erotic sight. Marta's red bottom wriggles but cannot escape the black plug wedged between her bright red cheeks. On her upper torso, the Trainer acts like a harness, surrounding her breasts, revealing more than it conceals.

Perhaps when we are in my quarters, I will keep my Tribute naked but for the Bride Trainer. Every morning, I can design the Trainer into a new formation that plugs her ass or even her mouth, and frames her breasts and punished bottom. My cock hardens at the thought.

For now, I command the Bride Trainer to attend to my Tribute's breasts. Thin tendrils stream from the main part of the harness to encircle her nipples. The tendrils tighten, pinching them. Marta writhes, her hands flying to cover her breasts.

"Hands above your head," I order. Instead of restraining her, I wish to train her to present herself willingly for punishment. I remember a phrase in one of my favorite manuals by Tymber Dalton. Or was it Maren Smith? "You are bound by my will," I intone.

Her chest heaves, her pupils darkening. Slowly, she obeys, stretching her arms up over her head. The movement causes her back to arch slightly, which pushes up her breasts.

"Good girl," I praise her, and reward her with another round of spanking. She still twitches and winces as I punish a particularly sore spot of her rear, but other than biting her lip against her adorable gasps and squeaks, she behaves.

I send the instructions to the plug in her bottom. It widens slightly and she moans, pink cresting on her cheeks. Her bottom has heated to a fever burn. I can sense it through the bond, and although her rear throbs painfully, it has awakened arousal in her lower half.

I could so easily push apart her legs and sheath myself inside her, and soon, I will. But first...

"Well done." I let her legs down. She shrieks as her sore flesh touches the bed. Before she can roll away, I reach forward to wind a hand in her hair and guide her to her knees in front of me. She looks up at me almost gratefully. It will be a while before she sits comfortably. Her cheeks are flushed, and while there's no sign of tears, her eyes are half closed, almost sleepy with surrender.

I keep hold of her thick brown hair and step closer. "Now it is time for you to thank me for your punishment."

My suit separates, revealing my erect member. Her dark brown eyes widen as my *seela* burst forth, stretching and straining towards her face.

* * *

Marta

ARKDHEM'S COCK bobs in front of my face, its flared head moving in its alien manner. This penis is porn-sized, but that doesn't take into account the extra appendages—namely the large flange of his prime *seela* that's waving in front of me, almost brushing my forehead. Then there are the tiny tentacles, their suckers end-upturned, as if seeking my face. Sure enough, as he steps closer and I prepare myself to take him in

57

my mouth—exactly the way the heroines in the naughty books I read thank their Doms for punishment—the *seela* latch on to my face and pull me forward. I keep my mouth open, and his length glides over my tongue. His salty meatiness fills my mouth. He groans, and I moan around him.

He cradles my head, studying how I take his cock. He threads his fingers into my hair and my scalp registers a bit of tension followed by a sharp tug. But the slight pain of hair pulling only sends a flash of pleasure to my pussy. I don't know how my wires got crossed—pain is pleasure, and pleasure is so intense that it hurts—but they did, and it works.

I raise my hands to steady myself, but remember him ordering me to be bound by his will. The phrase was hot enough to make me come, so I box my arms behind my back like a good little sub.

"Good girl," he murmurs, and I melt into a puddle. I open my mouth wider and accept him, stroking my tongue along his length, closing my eyes as his prime *seela* brushes my forehead. The tentacles on my face suck harder. As I bob my head up and down his length, the *seela* pop on and off. I'm going to have hickeys after this, all over my face, but I'm not mad about it.

Arkdhem guides my head for the first few times I take his length deep, but mostly lets me control the pace. But he's still in control. I kneel before him, the plug filling my ass. The Bride Trainer harness around my chest tightens, pinching my nipples. My pussy is dripping on the floor.

He steadies my head again. On instinct, I take a deep breath, and let him plunge my head down on his cock. He curls over me, grunting as he makes me swallow his sword. When he pulls out again, I'm gasping, tears running down my face. He thumbs them away reverently.

Then he thrusts deep into my mouth again. I relax my jaw and let him dominate me. The *seela* whip about my face, brushing my jaw and suctioning on, helping me hold position. Arkdhem's hips surge forward until his prime *seela* covers my eyes. He judders uncontrollably until, with a grunt, he empties himself down my throat. He immediately pulls out with a gasp, catching my chin to make sure I'm okay.

"Good girl," he murmurs, wiping away my tears. He seems almost fascinated by them, secret sadist that he is.

I lick my lips and look up at him. My ass is burning, my pussy is throbbing, and my clit wants attention, but satisfaction at pleasing him spreads through me in a warm glow.

He lifts me and positions me on my hands and knees on the bed. I settle in, expecting him to remove the plug and reward me. But he presses into my pussy. I gasp as both the plug and his cock fill me. The *seela* are active again, the long flange of the prime *seela* brushing my burning ass cheeks, and the smaller tentacles suctioning onto my chastised bottom.

Arkdhem seats himself fully in my pussy. His groin rubs the heated skin of my backside, making me groan. At the same time, little shivers of pleasure run through me at the full feeling. The Bride Trainer bits on my chest clamp tighter onto my nipples, but the pinching pain is lost in the overwhelming storm of sensation.

Arkdhem winds a large hand in my hair, tugging my head back. "Do not come," he orders, even as he starts thrusting hard enough to make my breasts bounce in the Bride Trainer harness. His groin slaps my ass, igniting the sting of the spanking all over again. I grip the bed blanket and grit my teeth, trying to hold off my orgasm. Arkdhem's hips slow their rhythm, and it's almost worse, because every time he bottoms out in my pussy, he grinds against my clit.

"Arkdhem," I gasp, and he pauses. I pant, so grateful that he's let my orgasm subside.

The butt plug filling my ass shifts, and I realize Arkd-hem's tugging on it, pulling it out slightly and pushing it back in. He's essentially fucking me in the ass with the plug.

Arkdhem resumes fucking me slowly. His cock drags over my G-spot and I drop my front to the bed, too weak to hold myself up anymore. My orgasm is rising, a bright blaze in my mind. It's so close, a huge tide I can't possibly hold back.

"Arkdhem, please," I beg.

"Call me 'Master,'" he orders, and when I do, he bucks his hips and orders, "Come."

And I do, sobbing happily into the bed, practically insensate.

When I come back to my senses, I think I might have fallen asleep again for a bit. I feel groggy. Befuddled.

Thank God for alien nanotech, because I'm pretty sure my pussy should be raw and chafed at this point. Unfortunately, the nanotech doesn't seem to be doing anything for the state of my ass.

Ouch.

Reaching back, I touch my hot cheeks and let out a hiss of breath. Spankings really hurt a lot more than I thought they would.

"I hope you learned your lesson," Arkdhem says sleepily, pulling me into his side and sliding his hand down to cup my buttock. The nanotech panties recede for his hand, so he can palm the full red mound, and I hiss again, squirming against him as the stinging pain flares.

"Yes, I did," I say. I learned that I'd better not get caught, because spankings aren't nearly as fun as my imagination had made them out to be. At least, disciplinary spankings aren't. I'd much rather have fun spankings. Though, the rest of it was fun... but sitting on my sore butt later won't be.

So, yeah. No more tempting spankings just for the sake of getting spanked.

"Would you like to have your tour of the ship now?" Arkdhem chuckles when I immediately sit upright, and then let out another little whimper as my weight presses my butt into the bed. *Ow, ow, ow.*

"Yes, I would," I say primly, pretending to be unaffected by both the renewed throbbing in my cheeks, and his amusement.

CHAPTER 7

Marta

Redressed in my gown, I accompany Arkdhem out the door and back into the hallway. As before, this corridor is empty.

"These are the sleeping quarters," he says, confirming my earlier guess. Nice to know I haven't lost it just because my brains have been fucked out.

As we walk through the corridors, headed who-knows-where, with my arm wrapped around his, Arkdhem starts to question me.

"What did you do on Earth?"

"You mean my job? That's what I spent most of my time doing." Because of its nature, I hadn't had much time for hobbies other than reading. My e-reader had been easy to take along with me wherever I went, and when I didn't have that, I could always access the app on my phone. I make a mental note to check out that pile of books that Arkdhem has, eventually.

"Yes. Dawn was a yoga instructor, and Pareena was a psychologist. What did you do?"

I remember that from the files that Frllil had on them. "I was an investigative journalist. I followed leads for stories, and reported on them." A sudden question pops into my head. Arkdhem brings up Dawn and Pareena a lot, and I kinda figured it was because they were the only two humans to join the Tsenturions so far, but now I realize he talks about them in a very familiar way. "Do you spend a lot of time with Dawn and Pareena?"

"Yes. I became their friend. And I was Dawn's guard when she first arrived." He smiles fondly, and I feel a little trickle of jealousy. "You will meet them when we return to the fleet." His smile flickers a little. Does he not want me to meet them? How close were they?

I don't get a chance to ask any of those questions, though, because I can hear many voices for the first time since we began walking through the ship.

"This is where we eat," Arkdhem says, leading me forward. The doors are open to a large room where many Tsenturion warriors are gathered, all of them seated, and eating. The food smells different, but that doesn't faze me. Everything I ate earlier was delicious and, as much as I traveled on Earth, discovering new foods was always something I enjoyed.

Though, I would also kill for some pizza right now.

"Do you want to go in?" he asks.

"I'm still full from earlier." I shake my head. Honestly, I probably could eat a little, but there's something intimidating about walking into a room full of warriors. Probably the fact that my butt is still sore and stinging slightly underneath my dress. I don't want them all to watch me try to sit down for the first time after my spanking.

And maybe I'm still feeling a little vulnerable because of that spanking.

Though, if anyone asked me, I would go to my grave denying it.

Satisfied with my answer, Arkdhem leads me on.

"Tell me more about being an investigative journalist. What is it?"

I laugh and explain as he continues to lead me down the corridor, telling him some of the stories that I uncovered, the prizes I won. A feeling of pride fills me as I remember how much I managed to do, but also sadness, because that's over. But, I remind myself, it could have been over because I died. Instead, I'm getting a new chance to make a difference somewhere else.

I just have to figure out how.

"This is our training area," Arkdhem says, and I pause in my stories to look into it. There are some half-naked Tsenturion warriors wrestling on a mat in the middle, and others doing what look like training exercises around the edges of the room. Damn. Maybe I don't need books for entertainment, I can just come here and watch this.

Not that I want any of them other than Arkdhem, but that is a lot of eye candy to enjoy.

"I do not understand," Arkdhem says after a long minute.

"What?" I tear my gaze away from the sexy display of alien flesh. If these guys could get to Earth, they'd have no shortage of volunteers to be Tribute. Ha!

"I do not understand. You regularly put yourself in danger so you could tell others the terrible things that some people were doing?"

That's actually a pretty good summation of my job; he understands it fine. "Yup."

"But why? Why put yourself in danger? You were not a soldier."

Oh, okay. Cultural differences. I can handle that. I had to navigate that all the time for my job, especially being a woman. Not to mention all the people back at home who didn't understand either, because they were worried about me, like my mother.

"Because I made a difference. My articles uncovered secrets, showing the true side of powerful people who needed to be brought down. Because of my articles, there have been companies who changed their policies to treat their workers better. Some, who were polluting the areas around them and making people sick, have had to pay to make them better, and some of them have gone out of business since then. Governments have changed their laws. I wasn't just uncovering the truth, I was making a difference and bringing about change to the world—good changes that helped people." My sadness over no longer having that rises again, but I push it down.

There's nothing I can do about it. Someone else will have to help them now. Hopefully, I'll be remembered for the good I did before I disappeared. I look up and realize that Arkdhem is staring at me.

"What?"

"You are even more amazing than I knew."

I can't tell him what those words meant to me—not that I'm given the time. His mouth descends on mine, kissing me almost desperately, and the next thing I know, I'm swung up into his arms. He's carrying me against his chest like we're on the cover of a romance novel, and rushing me back to his quarters while I giggle madly.

It's amazing my vagina hasn't caught fire from all the friction yet, but it hasn't.

The doors to Arkdhem's quarters glide open and the next thing I know, I'm bouncing onto our big bed. I yelp as my chastened cheeks touch the blanket. I'm still sore from the spanking.

I flip over to my hands and knees and start to crawl up

the bed but my big gold mate grasps my ankles and pulls me back down. There's a flutter in my pussy at the sight of him towering over me in his full armor. His gaze is hot and intent on mine as he drags me down the bed and parts my legs. I try to plant my feet into the mattress to push my hips up and get the pressure off my poor bottom, but he maneuvers me onto my back and down to the edge of bed where he's kneeling. His palms cup my rear cheeks, and he squeezes. I whimper but can't deny how the sting awakens my arousal. My pussy is already slick, ready for him. He wedges himself between my knees and tosses up the filmy garments that he dresses me in to wear out of the room. Something rips and he grunts, almost growling as he tears the rest of it out of the way.

I'm flat on my back, abs tightening as I fold in half to watch him take control. My legs are spread wide around his lean bulk. The Bride Trainer flows away to reveal my pussy to him. His nostrils flare as he inhales my scent. I squirm, but his left hand comes to my inner thigh, holding me open. With his right, he spreads my labia with two fingers and leans in as if studying my open sex. I'm dripping.

"Master," I whisper, my voice gone husky. He hasn't specifically instructed me to call him 'Master' every time we're in the bedroom, but it's hot, and he definitely likes it. And when he's happy, he's more inclined to make me happy, right?

"Lie back," he orders.

I obey, raising my hands over my head in the way I know will please him. The move pushes up my breasts. My nipples are still sore from their earlier treatment, pink and puffy.

"Good girl," he purrs. His thumb strokes up my labia.

The Bride Trainer probes my ass lightly, and then more intently until it stretches my private hole. I moan. Arkdhem taps the hard plug.

"Soon, I will take you here," he promises. I reach down automatically to cover my ass, and he smacks my pussy.

My legs snap closed but the bulk of his shoulders is in the way.

"No, no," he says with a wicked smile. He really is a secret sadist. "Hold your legs open," he commands.

I fist my hands at my sides and force myself to relax as he palms my pussy, grinding the heel of his hand against my clit. His hand rises and falls, spanking me once, but not too hard. A forceful heavy petting.

I keep my legs open, my eyes wide on his.

"Good girl." His hand falls again, this time, giving me a harder slap. My legs quiver and I arch my back, gritting my teeth. I register the force of the smack, but the sensation is confused by the stimulation on my clit. "My obedient Tribute." He thrusts two fingers into my pussy. "It is time for more training."

* * *

Arkdhem

After only two tsencycles, I am impressed by how well my Marta has accepted her training. She has learned to hold herself open to me, her hands bound by my will.

Even now, she lies with her arms stretched overhead, open to me. Her nipples are red and puffy from the pinching of the Bride Trainer. The sight makes me want to lower my head and lap at the tortured buds to soothe them, giving her relief from the torment caused. I can't bring myself to regret causing her a small bit of distress. Her pussy grows so wet when I dole out small doses of pain, the bitter bite tempering the endless sweetness of our interludes. She responds so well to the precise pain and I live for her reactions: the widening of her eyes, the pink flush to her golden skin, the way she bites her plump lip or opens her mouth to release husky, full-throated cries.

This session will not be easy for her. I intend to test the limits of her body in the most delicious way. A body like hers was made to be worshipped and I intend to do just that, but push her to the limit of both pleasurable pain and painful pleasure that she can endure.

Luckily, I studied the manuals often, and know them well. My extensive knowledge will allow me to create an experience neither of us will forget.

To start, I order the Bride Trainer to form a thin thread between her nipples. I visualize the item I read about in the manuals until the nanotech creates what I want: a delicate chain connecting the pincher-like sections that claim her nipples. Once it's formed, I give it a light tug. Her body shudders with the new, shocking sensation, her back arching beautifully to take the pressure off her punished tender buds.

"Keep your arms above your head, bound by my will. And open your mouth," I order her gently, and place the chain between her teeth. If she jerks her chin up, it will pinch her buds even more, forcing her to be complicit in her own torture.

With her nipples taken care of, I lower myself down to study her pussy. The pink lips are plump and slick under the dark down. Her little pleasure bud is starting to peek out from under its fleshy hood. I thumb the apex of her folds, not quite touching her clitoris. She shudders again, this time enjoying my ministrations. But her movement jerks the chain leading to her nipples, and her sigh turns to a distressed squeak.

I cannot suppress my wicked smile.

* * *

MARTA

It's the smile that clues me in. If I had any doubts, that deliciously evil smirk wipes them away. Arkdhem's a fucking sadist. My poor pinched nipples are evidence of that.

I'd be more upset if he wasn't everything I've fantasized about: a cuddly and attentive daddy-ish dom who pampers me in and out of the bedroom, but turns up the strict when it's time for punishment. Or, in this case, funishment. Even with my bottom freshly spanked, my body is hot and eager for anything else Strict Alien Daddy wants to dish out.

I stare down my body at Arkdhem, still keeping my arms up. He touches my pussy lightly, and I tense to keep from moving too much and causing extra strain on my nipples. My body is already warming, my pussy dripping in anticipation of both erotic pain and pleasure.

The next thing I feel is the plug forming in my ass, sliding deep and growing thicker until it stretches my ass to the point where it's all I can think of. The temperature in the room has gone up ten degrees. I squirm slightly, then whimper as I remember what movement does to my nipples. Fuck.

Still grinning, Arkdhem spears my pussy with a long finger, turning it and stroking the inside of my wall, finding my G-spot. After a few moments of him massaging my inner tissue, waves of pleasure begin to ebb through my core. The sensation ripples out from the source in my belly.

He lays his mouth over my vulva and probes my entrance with his tongue, at the same time keeping up that steady, deep massage with his hooked finger.

I'm moaning around the chain in my mouth. The sensation in my pussy grows sharper and my head goes back automatically. The movement sends a fresh burst of pain up from my clamped nipples. I moan again, this time in protest.

Arkdhem chuckles and clamps down on my legs when I try to close them.

"This is part of your training," he says. "You're being so good, but a few more sessions, and you will be perfect. Keep the chain in your mouth," he orders. "And do not come without permission. I will only give it to you if you beg, but if you lose the chain from your mouth, you'll be punished."

Not fair! I grimace at him. He's going to do his best to make me come, and if I come without asking permission, I'll be in trouble. But if I open my mouth to beg, I'll lose the chain. He's diabolical.

"For punishment, I will spank your pussy," he continues.

At that, my body clenches, sending a fresh wave of heat through me. Apparently, I find the thought of a pussy spanking super hot.

"So what will it be, my Marta? Will you be a good girl? Or will you defy one or both of my orders?" His thumb finds my clit as his inserted index finger rubs my G-spot. Meanwhile, the plug in my bottom swells, filling me to the point where my pussy spasms with need. My spanked bottom throbs in counterpoint, and I whimper.

"Do you need me to tie you down?" he asks, sounding almost solicitous. As if he'd tie me down for my benefit.

"Nnnnh," I answer. I will keep my arms up myself. He trusts me to remain bound by his will, and for some reason, I don't want to disappoint him.

"What's that?" He cocks his ear closer.

Bastard. I grit my teeth and shake my head in a tight movement, so as not to pull my nipples.

Arkdhem's eyes gleam as he lowers his head to lick my clit again. It's all I can do to keep my arms stretched above my head. Between the pressure inside my pussy and the wet tongue on my outer folds, my orgasm is rising. Even the rough heat in my bottom adds to the intensity. I shake my head as if I can deny it, and the movement pulls on my nipples. The sharp tug short-circuits my synapses, tripping another swell of arousal. I grit my teeth and fight it, which only makes it grow.

Arkdhem pauses mid-lick. "Are you a good girl?"

I nod, ignoring the way this movement makes my breasts bounce with the clamp. I whine around the chain of my mouth, pouting down at Arkdhem.

It does no good. "Do not come until I say so," the big golden bastard reminds me. His tongue flicks my clit, and his finger twists deep in my pussy. I feel the entire galaxy rotate. In all my wildest fantasies imagining a heroine sexually tormented by a big alien, I'd never imagined this.

I make a strained noise that would be a 'please' if I were not so obedient in keeping the chain between my teeth.

This time, it works. Arkdhem rises, and removes his finger from my pussy. My orgasm still hovers close, but it's nowhere as imminent as it would be if he kept licking and probing me.

"Good girl. You've done so well." He plucks the chain from my lips. I'm relieved until I realize he's ordered the Bride Trainer to create another chain, this one forming a clamp he hovers right over my clit.

"No," I gasp. Too late. He attaches the clamp right to my clit. The pinch makes my toes scrunch. My poor, swollen clit pulses.

"Breathe," he advises me.

"You breathe," I snap back. "I can't believe you—"

He holds something to my mouth, and presses it between my lips mid rant. It's nanotech similar to the Bride Trainer, and it fills my mouth and flows around my head, forming a sort of gag.

"Asshole!" I mutter, but luckily the word is muffled.

"Shhh." Arkdhem taps the font of the gag, looking

pleased. I glare back at him. I'm filled in every hole. My nipples throb in their clamps. My belly is still tensed against the pinch on my clit, but the sensation isn't so bad. The sting competes with the stretched feeling of my full ass and the slight burn of my spanked bottom. If I had to rank the discomfort, in first place would be the inside and outside of my ass, then my pinched clit, and finally, my nipples. And then the gag, although it's more annoying than anything. It's preventing me from cussing Arkdhem out, which might prevent me from getting punished. So that's good, I guess.

"Beautiful," he breathes right on my pussy. "I should dress you up in this every day. You will wear the chain, the clamps, and the gag. Oh, and your plug. Nothing else."

I grumble behind the gag, even though the thought of that is sorta hot. All the sensations are mixing in my body, overflowing. Arkdhem strokes my pussy again, close to my clit, and the discomfort I tallied earlier disappears, swallowed up with the screaming need to come.

"I'd like to try something." He stands and goes to the wall. His body blocks the replicator, but I can tell he's creating something. Now what?

He comes back with a long, narrow, cane-like stick that ends with a tea bag shaped flap at the end. A replicated version of a riding crop.

"I have heard about this." He whips it through the air, and tests the leather flap on his leg.

He's gloriously naked now. With the riding crop, he looks like the alien version of a sadistic lord in an erotic Victorian novel. I had a rare precious few kinky historical books on my e-reader. Now, it seems, I will live one of the scenes.

Arkdhem taps the end of the crop on my breast, using it to prod my clamped nipple and nudge my clit. I can't tell whether the sensation is agony or ecstasy, but it doesn't matter—by some strange alchemy, it adds to my building orgasm.

Automatically, I bring my hands down to shield myself, and Arkdhem tuts. "Naughty girl. Hold position."

I obey. I bite down on the gag, trying to keep control of the coiling tension in my core.

"I should punish you for that," he says in an offhand manner. So arrogant. Just like a Victorian lord. "I wonder… can you keep your arms up when I do this?" He touches the crop to his lips. I tense. The crop falls right onto my pussy.

WHAP!

I seize up but don't move my hands. The jolt makes me jerk, and my breasts bounce.

"Well done," Arkdhem says thoughtfully. "Two more."

WHAP! WHAP! He doesn't give me time to brace. But it's nice to get them over with.

"Very good," he purrs. "You deserve to be rewarded."

He gives a regal nod, and nanotech streams from somewhere and bind my ankles and my wrists. Probably not a good sign.

Once I'm fully tied down and helpless, Arkdhem checks the bindings, and paces to the end of the bed. I get the feeling he's fulfilling a particular fantasy.

"So lovely." He prods my pussy with his crop. He leans back as if waiting to enjoy the show.

At some silent order, the clamps on my nipples and clit open and fall away.

"Nnnn!" I shriek behind the gag. It's too late. The blood rushes into my tender buds and it's no use, the orgasm I've been holding back is now a tsunami of sensation. It sweeps over me, making me shake. My ass clenches around the plug with each breath-stealing wave, but my pussy aches to be filled. It's too much sensation, and not enough.

It wrecks me. If I wasn't bound, I'd roll into a ball. Tears leak from the corners of my eyes. I'm gasping around the gag —and suddenly, it's melted away. I let out a final, keening cry. Arkdhem's eyes slit. He's watching me like a connoisseur who's just been presented with the masterpiece of his life.

Fucking sadist.

And I realize what I've done.

"I didn't tell you to come," he says, and taps the crop against his palm. He kneels between my legs and brings his hand down on my pussy. Hard.

SMACK!

I jerk in my bounds, and howl. My poor pussy is going to be as pink as my ass.

The crop nudges my labia, stoking the fire that's starting to flicker to life.

WHAP! The next blow is from the crop, and it jolts my clit. Unbelievably, a fizz of sensation shoots through me. It's almost like a mini orgasm. Warmth is growing in my belly— the firestorm growing.

Arkdhem grins as if he knows what's putting the disbelieving look on my face. He alternates spanking my pussy with the crop and his left hand until I'm panting.

Then he taps the crop over and over on my labia, while thrusting a finger inside to find my G-spot again.

"Master!"

"Beg," he orders, and I do, in a rush of words, "Please. Please, I'll do anything, just let me come—"

He tosses aside the crop and goes to his knees. His mouth seals on my punished pussy. His tongue plunges into my entrance. Lips, tongue, fingers, it's all too much. Another finger fills me, and he stops tonguing me long enough to command, "Come."

His mouth fastens over my clit, and sucks. I come so hard, white stars burst behind my eyelids. I arch off the bed, straining in my bonds. My feet scrabble against the sheets. I ride the tight crest of the orgasm, and crash into another one.

And then he's stretched over me, gliding into my sopping pussy with one hard thrust. He fills me perfectly. With the stretch and burn inside and outside my ass, it's almost too much.

"Come," he orders. "Again." And I do. My pussy milks his cock and he speeds the rhythm of his hips, an intense look on his face. His thrusts rock my body. I'm stretched between the restraints, fully open to him and unable to resist the relentless pounding. The glide and burn is just what my next orgasm needs to start building.

"It's too much," I moan. "I can't—"

"You can. It is my will. Come for me, my heart. Let me feel your pussy squeezing my cock."

I scream and sob as another orgasm is wrung from my body, leaving me exhausted and completely satisfied.

Damn. I want to hunt down whoever gave Arkdhem the bride manuals. Best and worst present ever.

CHAPTER 8

*M*arta

In the following days, Arkdhem and I act like newlyweds on a honeymoon. In this case, the groom being a seven-foot alien warrior with armor that can change color and retract at a thought. Arkdhem shows me around the ship, and I meet several more of the officers. I'm really eager to meet the other two Tributes, but until we rendezvous with their ship, I settle into enjoying my new existence as a Tsenturion mate. When Arkdhem is on duty, I hang out with Medik, or simply stay in my quarters and sleep. I'm usually wrung out from the white hot sessions and sexual appetite of my Tsenturion warrior. Of course, Arkdhem wants to mate as much as possible—he hasn't gotten any in a thousand years. And I'm all too happy to accommodate him.

"Let's talk about the Tribute Program." We're in the bath, soaking after another marathon sex session where he tied me to a specially designed piece of furniture and used the Bride Trainer to edge me for what felt like hours. He finally forced me to come over and over with a plug in my ass. I fell asleep and woke up sticky—hence the bath.

"What do you want to know?" he asks.

"So we're just supposed to repopulate the entire Tsenturion race?"

He grins. "Do you have an objection to that?" His hand moves to casually cup my breast. His palm rubs my tender nipple, and even though he just made me come so many times I begged him to stop, pressure builds in my pussy at his touch.

"No." In this moment, I do not have an objection to it at all. His smirk turns smug, because he knows it. "Who came up with the plan? The Jabol, or Medik?"

"The Jabol approached us with the plan. And the High Commander approved."

He shifts slightly, removing his hand from my breast. He tenses up when he talks about High Commander Gavrill, and I'm not sure why.

"Hey." I scoot closer to him. "Is something going on between you and the High Commander?"

"What?" He regards me with a look of surprise.

"You tend to look uncomfortable when you talk about him."

"Before I left to retrieve you, we had a… misunderstanding. But it will soon be resolved."

"Misunderstanding? Does it involve me?"

"You are entirely too intelligent, my Marta."

Which isn't an answer. I press myself to his side, and he puts an arm around me.

There must be a healing serum in this water, because my sore ass and pussy already feel better. A few more minutes, and I'll be ready to jump Arkdhem again.

But first: answers.

I touch his knee, admiring how the water droplets make the golden surface gleam. "I can tell you're upset about something you're keeping from me. You can't hide your emotions from me —I'm a pro at it, and I can spot it when someone else is doing it."

"You do not hide from me."

"You're the only one," I insist. "I've opened up more to you than to anybody."

"Marta." He closes his hand around my wrist. I let myself be drawn into his lap, straddling him. It feels so good to be close to him, to have his naked skin gliding over mine. I've never felt so safe with anybody in my life.

"You can share with me," I say, leaning back to look him in the eye. "I've shared with you." And I have. Over the past few days—or daycycles as they're called on the ship—I've shared everything about my life. It's amazing that I feel so comfortable opening up to someone I've just met. But maybe that's a side effect of almost dying.

I told him about all my work and my past life, the dangerous situations I've been in. How I felt like I had to risk my life over and over, otherwise I'd be letting my father's legacy down, but at the same bearing the guilt of making my mother worry all the time.

I've bared myself emotionally and felt more naked with Arkdhem than with anyone else. But he accepted it all. I will do the same for him.

"In all my years as a soldier, I've obeyed my High Commander's every order—but one. But one act of disobedience is enough to mar my record. I hope, in time, I will be able to make amends."

What order did you disobey? It's on the tip of my tongue to ask, but he squeezes my bottom—which still has some soreness—and says, "You were asking about the Tribute Program." He's changing the subject, but I let him because I want to hear more. I make a mental note to ask him more about Commander Gavrill later.

"The Commander didn't tell the whole crew about the Tribute Program at first. We did not have much hope of finding compatible mates. The Jabol believe humans and Tsenturions share a common ancestor. But we didn't know whether the tests they ran at a distance were accurate until we acquired the first Tribute."

"But now you know we're compatible?"

"Yes," he says simply. Which doesn't do the subject justice. There are a lot of things to consider—human-alien compatibility, how the pregnancy will go, and also, just how many babies are we three Tributes supposed to have? There's more to this story.

But when I think of Arkdhem, alone and waiting for me all these years, my heart squeezes. I do want kids with him someday. Making them will certainly be fun.

"What do the other Tributes think of all this?"

He pauses before answering, his face thoughtful. He takes my questions seriously, which I appreciate. And he never seems to get tired of them, unlike my ex-boyfriends, who seemed intimidated by someone who was always probing for the truth that lay beneath the surface.

"There was an adjustment period," he says carefully. "For both of them. But now, they truly have come to care for their mates." He looks almost pained when he says it, and I can't stop myself from touching his jaw.

"I'm sure it was easy if their mates are as wonderful as you."

"Thank you, my Marta," he says. The tender look in his eye makes my chest ache in the best way. Sometimes I sense him watching me with almost reverence. I don't have to look at him to know he's thinking of me.

It's amazing to feel so connected to someone so soon—

and also a little freaky. I need to talk to someone about this--someone like me.

"I can't wait to meet Dawn and Pareena," I say. "When are we meeting up with them?"

The tension returns to Arkdhem's shoulders as he replies, "Soon." His suit/skin color has dulled slightly. He doesn't want to speak about this anymore. It's amazing how quickly I've picked up the minute changes in his expression and armor color, and can read his emotions that way.

"Okay," I say, so he'll relax. "No more questions." He wants to enjoy this moment, and honestly, so do I.

I trace the smooth edge of his shoulder. I'm not sure whether the hardened flesh is muscle or nanotech, or some combination of both. It's fascinating, and I make a note to go ask Rhodian more about the bio-nanotech. I wish I'd asked Frllil more about it, but I didn't realize exactly what it was until I saw it in person.

"My curious mate." Arkdhem cups my chin and nuzzles my cheek. I shift on his lap. In the water, his *seela* suction onto my hip, pulling me closer. In a few minutes, I'll be straddling him and riding him to another climax. But for now, it's nice to just cuddle. And explore.

Arkdhem's large hands slide around to cup my backside, steadying me as I mold my palms to his shoulders. His skin is back to a pale gold, darkening to a richer bronze lower down. Glimmers of color play over his skin under my fingers, like he's responding to my touch.

"What is it like?" I murmur.

"What is what like?" he asks, a slight uptilt to his lips telling me he's amused that I couldn't keep my promise not to ask questions for more than a minute.

I chase a bead of water down the smooth plane of his pectoral muscle with my forefinger.

"To have people know what you're feeling." The bead of

water disappears into a smooth groove between his pecs. I spread my palm over his chest, and a flush follows my hand: purple tinged with pink and a little gold, like a sunset. Talk about wearing your emotions on your sleeve.

"There are some among us who choose to hide their emotions," Arkdhem sounds amused. "I have always found it better to be honest."

"Do you?" I slide my hand lower and Arkdhem's abs flex, turning to steel. "Are you ever tempted to lie? To pretend you're feeling one way when really you're feeling another," I clarify.

He captures my hands, and holds them between us. "Is that what you do? Hide your emotions so you do not feel them?"

"No." I press our joined hands to my collarbone. "I feel my emotions. They're a deep, knotted mass in my middle." And they'll never be unwound.

He kisses my knuckles. "Perhaps I can help with that."

"I doubt it," I answer, my breaths coming quicker as his *seela* latch on to my inner thighs, positioning me more firmly over his cock. "But you can try."

Arkdhem cups the back of my head, cradling me close for his kiss. The *seela* are more insistent, tugging my hips down and suctioning over my labia until I gasp.

Arkdhem lifts me and the *seela* pop off in quick succession, sending tremors through my body. My mate rotates me so I'm bent over the side of the bath, with my elbows resting on the wide brim. Instead of tile, the bath is made of the same protean matter as the bedroom furniture. It feels softer, more like rubber, supporting my middle.

Arkdhem's hand threads into my hair and tugs my head back gently. My back arches, and I blink up at him from my contorted position. He runs his hand over my bottom and teases my labia with his fingers. I catch my breath, quivering in his hold. A few more strokes in the right spot, and I could come…

Smack! His palm cracks onto my wet skin. The water makes the sound echo louder than usual. He claps his hand on my opposite cheek. A few more hard smacks, then he swirls his fingers between my lower lips, stroking me lazily.

"You do not have permission to come," he informs me.

"But…" I whine, just like the bratty heroine I've always suspected it'd be fun to be.

Smack! "No. Behave."

A few more cracks to my bottom make me roll my lips between my teeth.

Stern bathtub Daddy for the win!

He takes his time teasing my clit and the sensitive pucker between my bottom cheeks, then sets about turning my rear pink. The water on my skin makes the spanking sting more, somehow. Why is that? Is it a physics thing? I could research it later—but then Arkdhem delivers a flurry of smacks that send every thought out of my head. My bottom is burning, sharing its heat with my pussy. I shift on my knees and Arkdhem tips me forward, so I'm even more helpless, bent over the bath with my rear in the air.

I'm gritting my teeth and trying not to cry out—no idea why it's a goal of mine not to make a sound, it just is—when the thought comes: *He's trying to make me cry.*

A little sound escapes me then. Not a sob, not really, but a little mew of protest? Surrender? My heart's melting a little, knowing that Arkdhem cares so much about my feelings, he's trying to give me an outlet. All the pain and tension and teasing my clit is meant to culminate in a catharsis of some sort.

I heave a sighing breath, and Arkdhem rubs my bottom. "That's it." He gives me a few hard swats that reverberate through me, shaking something loose in my insides.

A rush of emotion, not quite sadness but overwhelming in the same way, washes through me. The knot in my chest loosens, leaving me feeling lighter.

I realize Arkdhem has stopped spanking me. He lifts me back into his lap and cradles me in the water, letting me lean on one hip so I don't have to sit on my sore backside. The water is warm, and it feels good to curl up against my big strong mate.

"Do you feel better, my heart?"

"A little." I turn my lips down in a pout. "I didn't cry."

"That's all right." He hoists me closer. "Maybe next time."

"Maybe," I murmur. I'm sore and horny and a little bit sniffly, but mostly loving how close I feel to him. I stroke his sculpted bicep with my thumb. The water droplets glide across his golden skin, making it glitter. Under my hip, his cock is growing hard. I grin to myself. Now we get to the good part.

A flicker in the corner of my eye makes me turn. Someone's in the room with us. Where there once was empty air, there is now a nine-foot tall golden warrior standing in front of the bath, dressed in full Tsenturion armor.

My scream echoes around the bathing room.

The plates of the helmet retract, revealing the Tsenturion's face. He does not look happy.

"Arkdhem," the intruder growls.

I scramble to my feet before I realize the image before us is a little grainy and translucent. There's no one here—the figure in front of us is actually a projection.

Arkdhem rises in a rush of water. His large hand cups me protectively and he moves me behind him, inserting himself between me and the projection so he's blocking my view of the intruder with his impressive backside. Water streams down his back, sluicing in rivulets down the grooves of his muscles.

"High Commander. A minicycle, please. My mate and I require privacy."

I peek around Arkdhem's hip. So this is Dawn's mate, High Commander Gavrill. He looks twice as intimidating as he does in the Archives. His armor glitters with red on black so bright, it's enough to hurt my eyes. Between the face plates of his helmet, the High Commander's eyes are black.

This is not good.

"You have one hundred microcycles," the High Commander growls. "I will meet you in your quarters." The image flickers, and blinks away.

CHAPTER 9

rkdhem

I CLOSE MY EYES, a kind of grief and regret passing over me, even though I cannot truly feel either. Not when it comes to my Marta, my Tribute, my heart. I do not regret going to get her. I would make the same choice over and over again.

But the High Commander has been my mentor, the male I wanted to most impress, for so long that I cannot help but wish there had been another way. I knew I was going to disappoint him and had accepted it, but facing the reality of his censure hits me harder than I thought it would.

My chest aches, and my jaw clenches, along with my fists. It's a physical pain, one that I wish I could have avoided.

Hopefully he will understand when I am given time to speak with him directly. After all, he has his own Tribute. His Dawn. He knows the pull our mates have for us.

"What the hell was that about?" Marta's voice is shriller than before, and I open my eyes to see her standing with her arms crossed over her chest, staring at me with consternation and worry. I want to reassure her, but I am unsure how to.

"Marta, I must go. Remain here. I will dress and deal with this." I will explain myself to the High Commander and then return to explain myself to her. It is not that I meant to keep secrets from her, exactly, but though I would make the same choice, I am not proud of disobeying my commander, either.

"No." She jumps to her feet. "I want to go with you."

The earnestness in her expression, her immediate bravery, pierces my heart. Cupping her face in my hands, I lean in, stroking her cheeks gently.

"Please, my heart. Let me face this. It is me he is angry at, not you, and I would not have you bear the weight of his wrath for me."

"I don't understand…" Her eyes move to stare beyond me at the space where the projection invaded our privacy. Where the image of the High Commander had stood, interrupting our intimacy and casting judgment upon us. Something almost angry stirs in my breast, but I know I am the one in the wrong. No matter my feelings on the subject, I was given an order, and I disobeyed it.

I will accept my due punishment.

"What's going on?" Marta's eyes beg me for an explanation and I groan. There is no time, and yet I cannot leave her like this. But I have to.

"Marta… I have not been entirely honest with you." My jaw clenches at the words. "The High Commander has reason to be angry with me."

"Wha—"

"Stay here, and I will return to explain everything." I press a kiss to her forehead, still holding her face in my hands, before releasing her.

"No, wait—"

I can hear her call after me as I stride away, my armor plating my body as I move into the main room, the door to the bathing room sliding shut between us. The color of my armor is a dull grey, so different from the glittering gold that matches my skin that I have worn for so many days now. I flex my hands as I walk into my room, forcing my chin up as though I have nothing to be ashamed of.

False bravado, but right now, it is all I have to cling to.

I sincerely doubt my Tribute will be overly long in joining us, and I hope to get as much of my dressing down over with as possible before she does.

Thankfully, the High Commander's projection is already there, waiting for me. Odd to be thankful for that, since the very sight of him sends a small quiver through me. I feel like a young child, facing his disappointed father after disobeying him. It is not a comfortable feeling.

His eyes flash at me, jaw clenching as I stand in front of the projection and salute him. The High Commander wastes no time in chastising me.

"You were given orders to remain planet side and take control of the fleet in my absence. You abandoned your post and ended up light cycles away, on the edge of Jabolian territory. Explain yourself," he demands. Every word feels weighty with his tightly leashed anger, and it is all I can do to keep my own composure.

"I received word from the Jabol that my Tribute was ready." I stand straight at attention, looking him in the eyes, despite my impulse to drop my gaze. "So I went to retrieve her. You did tell me the next Tribute would be mine."

The High Commander's suit darkens to an inky indigo, flashing with streaks of red, indicating the depth of his anger.

"I did not tell you to disregard your duties." He snarls the words. "You didn't even send word. We could have been trapped on that planet. We could have needed your help and you would have been gone. You deserted your post when you should have waited—or, at the very least, *contacted me* so I could make the decision. You were *not authorized to do so.*"

* * *

MARTA

I scramble out of the bath, feet sliding on the tiles. I'm butt naked and, unlike Arkdhem, I can't just mentally signal my skin to grow some wicked cool Tsenturion armor. Too bad. It would be nice to be able to think a thought and be dressed that quickly.

By the time I've located a suitable robe that's not completely see through, Arkdhem is out in the office like area of his quarters. The projection of the Commander seems even bigger out here, dominating the spacious room. Is it life sized? If so, the Tsenturion Commander is huge.

The High Commander's projection crosses his arms over his armored chest. He's even wearing his helmet—and a few wicked looking spines protruding from it make him seem even bigger.

"You were out of communication range, and I did not want to disturb you on your honeymoon," Arkdhem replies smoothly. His armor is fully plated but without any the threatening protrusions the High Commander is displaying. There is something about his stance that hovers between defiant and conciliatory, like a teenager trying to convince his parent not to ground him after sneaking out of the house. I should know, I've looked the same way plenty of times. "I believed time was of the essence, so I did not follow protocol. You are the one who believes the Jabol are not to be trusted. Rather than leave her in the hands of a potential hostile force, I placed Corin in command, and went to retrieve her."

Wait, what? Hostile force? The Jabol aren't to be trusted?

Surely not. Frllil is one of the least hostile and unthreatening creatures I've ever met. Well, other than having the ability to snatch human women from Earth and then train them to be alien brides.

Hm.

Okay, they might have a point, when it comes to Earth women, but how the heck are the Jabol potentially hostile to the Tsenturions? That goes against everything I learned in Frllil's archives.

"We don't know if the Tribute was under threat," the High Commander grinds out.

"We didn't know if she wasn't," Arkdhem replies. "Especially if the Jabol discovered that we have had contact with the Vgotha."

What... they what?! The species who destroyed theirs?

My head is spinning this way and that, as new information collides with my desire to know what the hell is going on with my personal life. I've never had my personal life interfere with a story lead before, since I never had a personal life worth anything to me. It's both startling and unnerving for me to realize that I'm as invested in Arkdhem personally as I am in knowing what the hell is going on.

The commander grunts in begrudging concession. The spines on his helmet lower a few inches, and his face plate retracts fully.

"Arkdhem." The commander's voice is low and tired. He sounds like he's talking to a friend. "You should have followed protocol and told me. We were in communication range thirty five point nine percent of the time."

"I couldn't risk my Tribute," Arkdhem says, a tinge of sadness in his voice. For the first time, he looks away, casting his eyes downward, and my heart goes out to him. He looks so sad and I realize that this is more than a soldier being chastened by his commander... I might have been pretty on the mark with my comparison of him as a teenager to his dad. He cares about what the High Commander thinks of him, as more than just his superior officer. "If it were Dawn, you would have done the same." There is a pleading note to his voice.

Dawn is High Commander Gavrill's Tribute. It's a good argument, but the male shakes his head regretfully. His shoulders roll, and then the commander's mask is back in place. The dynamic between them has shifted again, from personal to professional, and fear strikes through me.

This is a military society, after all, and it sounds like Arkdhem disobeyed orders. What kind of punishment do they have for that? What are they going to do to him?

"You will face disciplinary actions for your desertion of duties." If there is a note of regret in the High Commander's voice, it's hard to hear. I bite my lip, watching the scene play out before me, not sure if it will help or hurt if I speak up.

Arkdhem brings his fist to his chest in a formal looking salute, bowing his head. "I expected nothing less."

"We could have been attacked and you left us helpless. We could have had need of all our forces, and you not only abandoned your post, you took others with you, none of them aware that they were aiding you in your desertion. You used their ignorance for your personal benefit. I cannot let these actions pass without punitive measures. The crew will need to be informed of the private orders I gave you, and the reason for your discipline explained."

"I will accept my punishment," Arkdhem says. His eyes remain on the projection of the High Commander but his hand extends to me. I shoot from my spying spot, holding my robe closed with one hand so I don't flash everyone, and take his hand with my other. Arkdhem folds me into his large body, my back to his front. His palm splays over my chest, pinning me against him and helping keep my robe closed.

"Marta is worth it. She's worth everything. The Tributes are our future, but Marta is even more to me than that."

There's a long pause. The High Commander is so still, he may as well have turned to stone. Then his gaze flickers to the right and down. For a second his face softens, transforming so completely, my heart stutters.

Then his gaze returns to Arkdhem and turns black once more. "Do not attempt to run. We will lock on to your location and we will be there in microcycles."

This time, the projection doesn't fade, but merely blinks away.

I clutch at Arkdhem's arm around my chest, needing his closeness while I marshal my thoughts. I shimmy to face him and hook my arms around his shoulders.

"Disobeyed only one order, huh," I say to break the ice. "You might as well tell me everything. I'm going to find it out anyway, and I'd rather hear it from you."

"Very well." Arkdhem sighs. "I shall."

Two minutes later, he has moved us to sit on the bed. He insisted I change into a new outfit, a long tunic over flowy pants. The fabric covers me a lot better than the robe or any of the flimsy dresses I've worn before, so I'm not complaining. After the way the High Commander saw everything, I wish I had some armor of my own. I mean, I was already wishing for armor, but that really solidified my desire.

In short sentences, Arkdhem explains what he has done: how the High Commander privately commanded him to keep orbit around the planet where he and Dawn were honeymooning, and how Arkdhem decided to deliberately disobey his directive. It might seem like such a small thing, after a lifetime of good service, but I spent a lot of time around the military when I was chasing stories on Earth, and even more time around cartels where disobedience didn't mean punishment or dishonorable discharge, it meant death.

"So you were supposed to stay at your post and you left?" I clarify, rubbing my forehead. There has to be a way out of this for him, but that is so cut and dry when it comes to the military types that I'm not sure what I can come up with.

"You were too important. I could not leave you in the hands of the Jabol. Even if—" he breaks off what he's saying and shakes his head. "That is not important."

"It seems important to the High Commander."

A flash of navy in Arkdhem's suit catches me by surprise.

"Gavrill already has his Tribute," Arkdhem growls. "What right does he have to deny me mine?"

Whoa, that's a lot of bitterness. I want to probe deeper, but I sit quietly, waiting for him to keep explaining.

He blows out a breath. "And now I'll be called to atone for my crimes. But it is worth it. He kneels before me and clasps my hands. "Anything is worth it for you."

"How will you atone?" What I'm really asking is how bad the punishment will be. It didn't seem like the High Commander was going to be calling for his death or anything, but I have no idea what kind of 'disciplinary actions' an alien race might deem justifiable.

"I'll be judged by the High Commander and a panel of my peers, who will decide my punishment."

"Not the fun type of punishment, I'm guessing."

His lips jerk into a tiny smile at my attempt at a joke. "No, my heart." There's a thud in the corridor, and his body tenses. "They are coming."

I grab his hand as he stands. We'll face this together. No matter what.

The rhythmic thuds grow louder until the sound stops outside the door.

Without Arkdhem's permission, the door glides open and a bunch of warriors march in, each in full armor. At the front of the squad is the High Commander. Like the rest of his soldiers, his helmet covers his face.

I knew this was going to happen, and it's still hella intimidating. Arkdhem squeezes my hand. Gavrill's helmet swivels down as he notes our hands are joined. "Release the Tribute."

I grab Arkdhem's wrist with my free hand before anyone can say anything else. "No," I say. My voice quivers a little, so I firm my abs and project properly. I try to slide in front of Arkdhem, to shield him with my body, but he maneuvers me back so that he's shielding me instead. That still doesn't stop me. "I'd like to know what's going on." I say it firmly, hoping that the whole Tribute thing means I get some leeway, and that I'm not about to face my own punishment for disobeying the High Commander.

"This warrior has committed treason and abandoned his post. He will now be disciplined by the High Command."

To my shock, Gavrill sinks to one knee so he's closer to eye level with me. "He will not be harmed, Marta Flores Romero; simply held for his crimes. If you will come with us, we will make sure you have not suffered any mistreatment." His helmet retracts a little, letting me see his eyes, which have lightened to a deep navy. Looking at me, his expression seems almost... kind.

So the High Command thinks Arkdhem abused me as well as disobeyed orders.

"I'm fine. I prefer to stay with Arkdhem."

"Babe, I've got this." A human slips in from the hall and pokes her head out from behind the warriors. She's pale and slender, her long brown hair pulled back into a sleek ponytail.

She's half the size of the warriors, but they all step aside for her, giving her a clear path to the High Commander.

Gavrill rises and takes her hand much like Arkdhem took

mine. Large armored warriors and small humans—we're mirror images of each other.

This must be Dawn, Gavrill's mate. When she tilts her head to study me, a jolt runs through me. It's been a while since I've seen a human being, and although Dawn looks tiny compared to the warriors, she's actually a few inches taller than me.

"Hi," she says in her American twang. "I'm Dawn. Pleased to meet you." Her mouth twists. "I wish it was under better circumstances."

Better how? Better as in: 'we haven't just been abducted by aliens,' or, 'your mate isn't accused of treason and they're not going to separate him from you.'

"Sure," I say.

"If it's all right, we would like to talk to you separately," Dawn continues while her mate and the other hulking warriors stand quietly. It's kind of adorable how they're letting her take charge. I'd be amused if the moment wasn't so tense. "Look, I understand that you may not trust us yet. In which case, I'm asking Gavrill—I mean, the High Commander—if there's a way you can talk to us privately and still see Arkdhem. And he can somehow see you?"

She cranes her head up towards her mate. The soft expression is back on Gavrill's face.

"That will be difficult," he murmurs, "because I do not wish to put you and her anywhere near the brig. And that is where Arkdhem belongs."

"What if we use my tablet? Set it up so Marta can have a video link to Arkdhem?"

"That can be arranged." The High Commander touches Dawn's cheek and strokes it gently. "Thank you, my Dawn." She flushes a little, and nods. That doesn't seem scripted.

Dawn looks at me. "Marta?"

I hesitate because video can be doctored. Who knows

what sort of high tech these aliens have? But Dawn is making an effort.

"Okay," I say. "I'll accept that." I turn to Arkdhem.

"Go with the Commander's Tribute," he orders softly, and touches my cheek in a similar move to Gavrill's, and I flush just like Dawn did. Damn, I do feel something deep in my chest. Real human emotions.

I swallow. "Will you be all right?"

"As long as I am reunited with you."

"You will reunite us?" I ask the High Commander.

Gavrill nods slowly. "If that is what you wish."

Squeezing Arkdhem's hand one last time, I walk slowly to stand by Dawn.

"This way." She whirls, and I follow her from the room, looking back as the contingent of guards close around my mate.

CHAPTER 10

Marta

As I step out of the room alongside Dawn, I get my first really good look at her and manage to hold back a gasp when I see her rounded belly. Holy shit, she's pregnant! That wasn't in Frllil's files!

I can't help but wonder if he knows, and I have to squash the urge to call him on his comm-unit... especially after what Arkdhem said about not knowing if the Jabol are trustworthy. I don't know what's going on yet, so I shouldn't make any hasty moves, like make someone else's pregnancy announcement for them. That's a messed-up move back on Earth all on its own; out here, where entire species are at risk, it seems like it would be even worse.

"Are they going to hurt him?" I ask Dawn, instead of commenting on her stomach. Also messed up back on Earth is assuming a woman is pregnant. She looks like she is, but for all I know, she's gained a bunch of weight in just one area of her body that happens to be her stomach, thanks to alien cuisine. So I do not comment on the pregnancy until she tells me something herself.

I don't know if I can trust her answer, but I can't think of anything else to say to him.

"No. But they will discipline him." She gives me a sympathetic grimace when I glance back over my shoulder. I can't see Arkdhem, but I can see the group of Tsenturion warriors walking away from us, going in the opposite direction down the hall, and I know he's at the center of it. "I don't know what that means though. Gavrill has yet to explain, especially since I'm pissed as hell that he's going to punish Arkdhem in the first place." She makes a face. "I think what he did makes perfect sense. Gavrill's just got a stick up his ass sometimes."

Yeah, from what I know about Dawn, she would not be on board with the whole military view of things. Despite everything, I can't help but smile. Gavrill must have his hands full dealing with her.

"So, uh... did you have a good honeymoon?" I ask, since it appears that we've got quite a bit more corridor to go. I wouldn't think that I would be able to tell the difference between space ships, but at a certain point, I realize that we've left the ship I was on and are now walking down the corridors of a different one. The High Commander and his warriors must have boarded our ship.

"Yes." She tosses her ponytail over her shoulder, smiling wryly. "At least, up until the end. It was a bit of a surprise when Gavrill tried to comm Arkdhem and got Corin instead. We cut our honeymoon short." She's still talking about Arkdhem's insubordination. "How are you doing? That might be kind of a silly question, considering, but..."

"Oh, I'm fine." I wave a hand. The sooner I convince everyone of that, the sooner I can be reunited with Arkdhem. I hope. The worried look she shoots me makes me think I have a lot of work left to do.

"Here." She gestures to the right of the curving hall. A door glides open as she approaches. "We can talk more privately in here." She sweeps her hand out, indicating that I should enter first. Inside is a simple, white-walled room that would look intimidating without the decor. A white, human-sized round table surrounded by chic salmon pink chairs, and a matching painting on one of the walls, makes the place look a little less like an interrogation room.

There's someone inside already waiting for us, seated at the table with her hands around what looks like a tea cup. A human. It only takes me a moment to recognize Pareena from the pictures Frllil had in his files, though she looks very different from the professional headshots he'd gathered from Earth.

Seeing her sitting there makes me think of her profession —she's a psychologist. Doctor Pareena Singh. Suddenly, the room seems a little more like the interrogation room I first likened it to. I press my lips together and turn to Dawn.

"Where is Arkdhem?"

"Probably already in the brig. Speaking of which—" She waves a hand at someone down the hall and when I look, there's a warrior walking up to us with a solemn expression on his face. Even though I know that's the usual expression for all of the warriors, my stomach still clenches a bit with worry.

Does he know who I am? Does he know what's happening with Arkdhem? Is that why he looks like that?

"Tribute Dawn," the Tsenturion says gruffly, not looking at me, and hands my guide what looks like a tablet. "They've set up the video feed."

"Thank you," Dawn says, handing the thing off to me as the warrior bows and walks away.

Hesitantly, I touch the screen and the tablet lights up. Unlike anything I had at home, there's no screen filled with options.

Instead, the display shows an image of Arkdhem standing

in a three-sided room. His armor covers his body and his hands are fisted at his sides. He's standing rigid like he's up against a wall. The air in front of him ripples a little—it's a see-through pane made of something like liquid glass. There's room enough for him to walk back and forth and there's even a bench for sitting, but instead, he stands there, motionless, staring at nothing.

I want to hug him so badly.

"What happens now?" I can't take my eyes off my mate.

"There, he'll wait for sentencing. But first, the High Commander will want to talk to you. Now, get inside, Pareena's been dying to meet you." She gently turns me by the shoulders and pushes me into the room. I don't bother resisting. My brain feels frozen and I don't know what to do, so I let her guide me. For now.

"Hi," I say as I walk in, my gaze meeting Pareena's. She smiles at me warmly, but it doesn't reassure me. I'm not sure anything could right now.

"Hi Marta. I'm Pareena, and I'm also the ship's counselor. How are you doing?" It's the same question Dawn asked me, but coming from a psychologist, it feels a lot more loaded. She gets to her feet and holds out her hand for me to shake. It's harder to take my own hand off of the tablet than I would have expected, but I make myself do so.

"Um. Fine? I mean, other than being separated from my mate and not knowing what his punishment is going to be. That sucks a lot." I glance down at the unchanging image of Arkdhem.

"I can only imagine," Pareena says sympathetically. "If it helps, Dawn and I are totally on your side. Arkdhem is our friend, and we want to help. Is it okay if I ask you some questions?"

"Sure." What else am I going to do? And, even though I don't know her or Dawn yet, the fact that both of them say they want to help is my only hope. They're mated to the High Commander and the second-in-command of the fleet. If anyone can help me, it'll be them.

"Anyone want tea?" Pareena asks as Dawn and I settle into our chairs.

"Oooh, I do." Dawn jumps back up immediately, but Pareena touches her arm.

"You sit. Take a rest."

"I'm fine," Dawn says but relaxes back in her chair, stretching out her legs and rubbing her convex stomach. "Do we have any cookies?"

"Of course." In the corner, Pareena types into the replicator and returns with a tray set with teacups, a steaming tea pot, and a platter of cookies. She serves the tea and pushes the cookies right in front of Dawn. "These are as close to my favorite tea biscuits as I can make them."

"Thank you." Dawn takes two and shoves them into her mouth. I can't help but smile. Being around two other humans feels both odd and nice after so long with Frllil and then Arkdhem. I'm still eager to see Arkdhem again, but it's nice to see my own species again and be around familiar mannerisms. I grab a cookie of my own, though I nibble at it, rather than scarfing it down the way Dawn did.

"Now," Pareena turns her serene smile on me, "we can talk properly. We don't know anything about what's going to happen with Arkdhem unfortunately, but do you have any other questions?"

Oh boy, do I ever.

* * *

Arkdhem

. . .

I STAND IN THE BRIG, right up against the transparent wall. Beyond my prison, two guards stand at attention near the door. Soon, the High Commander will walk through and interrogate me further.

Every microcycle feels like an hour. They have fixed a tablet across from me. Every so often, it blinks on for a few microcycles to give me a few precious moments of Marta's face. She's sitting at a white table, eating and speaking with the other Tributes. There's no sound, just the images—and too soon, it blinks away. I don't dare look elsewhere, in case I miss that precious glimpse.

To stand here and watch my Tribute for only a few moments at a time is torture, although the High Commander did not mean it as such. I know he meant it as reassurance, to be able to see and know my Tribute is well. But any microcycle away from Marta is painful. My nose touches the fluid border between myself and the rest of the room.

The screen blinks on. There are Dawn and Pareena at a table on either side of my Tribute. Marta has a blank expression on her face but her eyebrows rise a little bit. Dawn is waving her hands as she speaks, almost knocking her beverage over. Pareena nods at whatever Dawn is saying, but keeps checking Marta's expression.

My Tribute is the most beautiful of them all.

When my screen blinks off, I am gripped with the pain of losing sight of her again. The worry over what will happen to her. Wondering why it is taking so long for my fellow warriors to come for me.

Logically, I know I have not been waiting long, but my patience is already wearing thin. Whatever discipline awaits me, I would rather get it over with.

Color crawls over my suit until it looks like it's broken. My emotions run one into the other. One of my shoulders is red, the other orange. The bright colors deepen to purple and blue. My lower half is black. The darkness is at my midriff, and it's rising, along with my frustration and grief.

It is not as though I wanted to betray my people. But I do not know where I would have made a different choice. For all the High Commander says I should have come to him, he has his own Tribute to protect. How could I trust that he would put her in danger in order to retrieve mine?

And he does believe the Jabol are dangerous.

He was willing to not only listen to the Vgotha, but he believes their tale that the Jabol enslaved them and destroyed Tsentur in order to secure our services as warriors when the Vgotha rebelled. Me? I am not so sure. The Vgotha are a worthy foe in battle. The Jabol? Not so much. I do not see how they could have done all of that. I do not think they could have fooled us for so long.

But I know the High Commander was taken in by their story.

I left the majority of the fleet to guard him and his Tribute while I retrieved mine. I deserted my post but... it is a new world. We are no longer purely military. Before Tsentur was destroyed, warriors would retire to become civilians before taking a mate. That is no longer the way things are done. Changes should be—need to be—made in order to accommodate our new circumstances.

Surely the High Commander and the others will see that.

The door glides open. I jerk my head up. I'm ready to face my high commander. But it is not the High Commander who drives into the room, but a warrior clad in black armor.

Bodgan.

My lip lifts in a familiar snarl. Out of everyone on the ship, it had to be him. We have never gotten along. He did not even want a Tribute, and yet he received Pareena anyway. I was so sure he could not deserve her, could not treat her appropriately, that I attempted to battle him for her.

Now, I am glad I lost, because otherwise I would not have my Marta, but I still do not think he deserves her.

He gestures to the two guards to leave, and they do. He approaches the open side of the brig and stops in front of the invisible current keeping me in.

"Hello, Arkdhem."

* * *

MARTA

"AND THEN THERE IT WAS! And I was like, 'Oh my god, those are tentacles!'" Dawn's arms flail and she opens her mouth in a mock scream. Pareena's giggling into her tea cup, and even I can't help but chuckle. Dawn is so funny and animated.

Pareena is more collected but she has some funny stories too. Apparently she'd thought her whole abduction and mating was a super sexy dream she was having. Which… I can't blame her, especially since she'd been in the hospital dying when she was taken.

We're on our third pot of tea, and the cookie plate holds only crumbs. We've talked about *everything.* I now know more about their mates' sexual prowess than I ever wanted to about anyone else. But it's informative.

What's weird is I'm oversharing as much as they are.

"The *seela* did throw me off at first," I say. My cheeks are hot with a blush, but I can't stop the words from spilling from my mouth. I can't remember having a gossip session like this since high school, but there's something therapeutic about it, and not just because Pareena is an actual psych. I used to chat with my editor about leads over drinks, but that probably didn't count as girl talk. My editor and I weren't close friends. Friends wasn't something I really excelled at, but Pareena and Dawn kinda feel like what I remember friends being like. "But now I like them. I'm not sure I could go back to regular peen. Not sure what that says about me."

"Once you go tentacles, there's no going back," Dawn quips.

"So glad I'm not alone." I swivel in my chair to Pareena. "How's the psychological evaluation going? Did I get an A?"

"You did fine," Pareena assures me, laughing. She's not like any psych counselor I've ever met, and I had to go to a few back on Earth after some particularly harrowing assignments—at my editor's insistence. I wish Pareena had been one of them. She's incredibly easy to talk to.

Dawn cackles. "Don't tell me she's normal."

"No more abnormal than the rest of us." Pareena rests her chin on her hands, still smiling. "But the really important thing is how you feel about Arkdhem."

I swallow hard. Feelings? Yeah, talking about sex I can do, but talking about my feelings? Suddenly, Pareena reminds me a lot more of the therapists I saw back home. I roll my eyes. "Does it matter? The sex is great. That's more than I had back on Earth."

"Do you feel like you have a connection to Arkdhem?" Pareena presses, the therapist side of her coming through a little more strongly now. But I have a lot of practice at avoidance.

"When his little *seela* suckers latch on to my pussy, I do," I say as crudely as possible. Pareena narrows her eyes at me, studying me like a bug under a microscope, and I get the feeling that she sees right through me. Which is not comfortable. I shift in my seat, avoiding meeting her gaze.

"Damn right." Dawn tilts her head. "Gavrill is coming." She sounds breathless.

A few seconds pass, and the door doesn't glide open. I can't tell how she knows her mate is on his way—if he even is. There's only one explanation, but it's one that Frllil had discounted in his notes: the full bonding of a Tsenturion male to his mate.

"Can you sense him?" Holy shit. They're hiding a lot from Frllil. Dawn's pregnancy. The full bond. And I've been so busy talking about hot alien sex that questioning them about the Jabol and Vgotha completely slipped my mind, which isn't like me at all.

Then again, it's not like I have a story deadline. Maybe that's why I'm so easily distracted.

"Yes," Pareena answers, because Dawn's mouth is still full of cookie, though she's nodding. "We can sense our mates. There's a sort of bond."

"Really?" For some reason, I don't want to tell them about the research I did on the Tsenturions and them. It seems a little bit like an invasion of privacy, for one, and for two, I want them to trust me. I can't decide what to tell Frllil myself until I have more information.

"Yes." Pareena leans over the table towards me. "Do you feel anything like that with Arkdhem?"

"No, but I'm not really a touchy feely sort of person. I prefer to look at things logically." The words trip off my tongue by rote. The same answer I gave over and over again to my therapists back home.

"So how do you feel about Arkdhem?" Dawn asks, getting up and moving towards the door, like she's getting ready to jump on whatever comes through it. She's that sure that her mate is on her way. It's both startling and worrying.

"I like him," I say, fiddling with my hair. "I mean, the sex alone—"

"Is it just the sex?" Pareena probes. "Or is there more?"

"I don't… I don't want him to be hurt. I'm worried about him with this whole discipline thing."

Under the table, I clutch the tablet. Last time I checked it,

Arkdhem was standing in the brig, staring out of the glass like he was hoping I'd appear before him. I know what he was hoping for because I was hoping for the same thing. But acknowledging it to myself was hard enough; sharing it felt impossible.

"I want to be with him," I say, after staring at the tablet in silence for several moments. That is the best I can do.

"That can be arranged," Pareena says. "We just want to make sure—"

The door glides open, and the High Commander strides in.

CHAPTER 11

M *arta*

The High Commander looks as intimidating as I remember, and I shrink back into my seat a little. Dawn, on the other hand, jumps right on him. He easily catches her, holding her against him and giving her a thorough kiss before letting her slide down his body.

Seeing them together messes with my brain a little. I want to dislike him for interrupting me and Arkdhem and then separating us, but seeing how gentle and caring he is with Dawn makes it kind of hard. I, of all people, know that people are more than one thing. They can be both kind and cruel, depending on the circumstances and how they view the person in front of them, but it's never been personal the way it is right now.

"Tributes," he greets us as he puts Dawn back on her feet. She leans into him happily, his arm wrapped firmly around her. I push my chair back to stand, and he signals me to stay seated. "Please, sit."

As he moves towards the table, my eyes fall to the tablet

in my lap. It looks like Arkdhem is talking to someone. A warrior in dark armor.

I trace Arkdhem's face on the screen with my finger. There's an ache deep in my gut. I miss him way more than is logical, and I can't help but wonder if the bond Pareena was talking about is part of it. If she and Dawn bonded with their mates, maybe Arkdhem and I really are bonded too.

Does that mean some of what I feel is him missing me?

"Babe, this table is designed for humans. Human women." Amusement laces Dawn's voice as the High Commander pulls out a chair and moves to sit down in it. I'm pretty sure I hear Pareena snicker, but it's too quiet for me to be completely sure.

"I will manage," Gavrill assures her. When he sits, it is kind of comical. I wait for the chair to creak and fall apart under his bulk but it doesn't. His knees poke up over the table. Like an adult sitting at a kiddie table. At any other time, I would have laughed, but I'm too nervous right now.

"Tribute Marta Flores Romero," he greets me. The formal greeting reminds me of Frllil.

"Please, call me Marta." It's a little hypocritical, since I'm having trouble thinking of him as anything other than 'High Commander' despite knowing his name, but being called by my full name like that is unsettling. I finally broke Frllil of the habit, I don't want to start all over again.

The High Commander glances at Dawn, as if asking permission, and she nods.

"Marta," he says my name carefully as if testing it out. "Do you understand the charges against Arkdhem?"

"Yes."

"And has Tribute Pareena explained the bonding?"

"I understand that I'm bonded in the way of your people to Arkdhem," I say slowly. What can I say to help Arkdhem? Not that I want him to avoid punishment. I just want him to be okay. "Or, if I'm not totally yet, I will be soon. Because the Jabol made sure I was compatible with him. Right?"

"That is correct." A new voice at the door makes me jump. I hadn't even noticed it opening, which doesn't say much for my survival skills. It's like I've forgotten everything I knew. Arkdhem fucked it all right out of my head. I need to get my shit together because all my instincts seem to have deserted me. The male standing there is different. Older. Softer in demeanor somehow, and he's not wearing armor like the rest of the warriors. "May I enter?" he asks, and Gavrill waves him inside.

"Marta, this is Medik, the Tsenturion's physician," Dawn introduces us.

"Hello," I say, and this time, I do get to my feet to shake his hand. He smiles in a friendly manner as he does it, completely comfortable with the human gesture, which makes me feel more comfortable with him immediately.

"Hello," Pareena greets Medik. Both she and Dawn are all smiles, looking at him like he's their golden alien grandpa.

"Dawn, Pareena. Marta," he greets us all and turns to me. "I have looked over your scans and report from Frllil, and assured Gavrill that you are in perfect health. Moreover you do not seem to have been mistreated." It doesn't escape my notice that he says the High Commander's name in a very familiar manner, and not at all like a subordinate.

"That is good," says the High Commander, turning to me, his expression softening. "But you should not have been put through this ordeal."

"I'm fine." If the High Commander were human, he might hear some of the warning and impatience in my voice. Apparently, Dawn hasn't taught him about the word 'fine' though, since he seems unperturbed, while Dawn and Pareena exchange a worried glance.

"I am glad you were unharmed. Of all our protocols, the

most important is the safety of our Tributes." He says the words with grave seriousness. What an interesting way to put it. Dawn rolls her eyes. Pareena looks like she wants to say something, but I beat her to it.

"I'm glad you have such strident protocols in place," I say with a straight face. Not sarcastic at all, nope, not me.

The High Commander seems to think I'm sincere. "Our protocols have kept us from devolving into chaos. That is why there are such strict consequences for those who break them."

I stiffen. Meaning: Arkdhem is in big trouble.

Gavrill continues, "Now, there is the matter of your bond. Medik has assured me we can break the nanotech. It will be difficult, but—"

"Whoa, hold on," I say, holding up my hand. I don't care if he is the High Commander and leader of an entire fleet, I'm going to interrupt his ass and find out what the fuck is going on. Break the nanotech? Surely it can't be that easy. Pareena and Dawn seem to think that being able to feel Arkdhem's emotions would be important. "If I feel what Arkdhem is feeling, does that mean we're bonded?"

"Yes." Pareena looks a little relieved. She shoots a glare at the High Commander, and Dawn has gone stiff beside him, looking upset. Not that he seems to notice. "Yes, that would be the bonding."

"It can still be severed," the High Commander says, his voice somewhere between firm and gentle. "We have not attempted it with a Tsenturion-human mating yet, of course, but for Tsenturions paired with an unsuitable mate—"

"Hold up." I raise my hand again. "You want to break us apart?" Both Pareena and Dawn are looking more and more upset, but that's nothing compared to how I'm feeling. I might not want to admit aloud how much Arkdhem already means to me, but I'll be damned if I let them take him away from me.

"Yes," the High Commander says. "Immediately, if you want."

I drop my hand and clutch the tablet in my lap, staring at him. "Why would I want that?"

"Once we break the bond, you will no longer be Arkdhem's mate." He says the words like that makes everything clear, and I suddenly feel very sorry for Dawn if this is an example of his listening comprehension skills. Has he not heard one thing I've said since he barged into mine and Arkdhem's lives? Beside him, Dawn is starting to wriggle, a dark look on her face. Pareena now has her arms crossed over her chest, and she's glaring at the High Commander.

They hadn't been lying about being on my side, and that gives me even more courage to defy the leader of an entirely alien species.

"I don't want a new mate." I say the words clearly. Succinctly.

"I know this isn't an ideal situation." His tone gentles a little, not that I care. "You have already bonded, but our protocols require—"

"Why can't I just remain bonded to Arkdhem?" I interrupt him again. I don't care about their protocols.

Gavrill's suit darkens to a blue that's almost black. His voice is stern when he says, "Arkdhem's crimes cannot be rewarded."

"She's not a reward, she's a person." Dawn looks like fire's about to shoot out of her eyes as she jerks away from her mate. I silently cheer her on as she slaps her hand down on the table. "Unless you think *I'm* a reward for good behavior? In which case, maybe we should break our bond, because I don't think forcing a woman to break her bond because *you* don't like it is good behavior."

The High Commander's suit flashes pure white. He reaches for his mate, but Dawn slaps his hand away, still glaring.

"High Commander, I thought we were past this," Pareena says in a quiet tone that holds as much anger as Dawn's outburst. "Tributes have their own emotions and desires, which are valid and must be treated as such, unless you want us to feel like objects and as though we aren't valued."

"Yeah, what they said," I add, crossing my arms over my chest and enjoying the panic rising in Gavrill's face as he faces a united front of furious human women. I don't even need to argue my point, Dawn and Pareena are doing it for me.

The Tsenturions want human Tributes? They're going to have to learn how to deal with us.

* * *

Arkdhem

"Bogdan," I say warily.

Bogdan's suit is glossy black as usual, but there's no sign of the bright gleaming stars that appeared after he bonded with Pareena. His helmet fully covers his face, and a forest of spines protrude from his armor. He looks ready to fight.

I'm standing right up against the shimmering barrier of the brig that's keeping me prisoner. As Bogdan comes to face me, my own armor starts to respond to his warlike stance. The nanotech bulks up, adding protective mass to my legs and torso. My helmet extends to cover my skull and jaw, but I don't allow it to shield my face.

"How was your honeymoon?" I ask in a bland tone.

"Terrible," he growls. "Thanks to you."

"So that's why you're in a bad mood." I tap my helmet. "Oh, no, wait, I forgot who I was talking to. You're always in a bad mood."

Bodgan continues like I haven't spoken. "Instead of a nice relaxing vacation with my Tribute, I ended up learning of your betrayal, and racing to hunt you down."

Racing? I'm flattered. But instead of goading him further, I try to reason with him. "It couldn't be helped. My mate was potentially in danger."

Bogdan scoffs. "A convenient excuse, but you and I both know you don't believe what the Vgotha have told us about the Jabol. The High Commander might believe your lies but I know the truth." He points a finger at my face, close enough to the barrier to make it ripple in warning. "You would have acted against orders and gone to pick up your Tribute whether or not she was in danger."

"It's true," I say. Why deny it? I think that the High Commander and Bogdan have been duped by the Vgotha. Dawn has resentment against the Jabol, and the Vgotha's story fed into that. But I also know that Bogdan now believes the Jabol to be our true enemies. "Would you not do the same for Pareena if she were in Jabol hands?"

"Do not speak her name!" Bogdan's roar reverberates around the brig.

So he's still touchy because I tried to seduce his Tribute. And I can't help twist the knife. "Perhaps that is why you didn't have a good honeymoon. Your Tribute senses that you do not truly care for her." Red streaks ripple through Bogdan's armor, but I continue. I don't have anything better to do, and my own anger and frustration have built and built and built while I've been waiting for whatever will happen next. Bogdan has always made a convenient outlet for such emotions, and I still do not think he deserves Pareena. "If you were truly worthy of her, you wouldn't have resisted bonding with her for so long."

"Be silent," he roars. His suit flashes red with anger, the color streaking through the deep black. "The only reason you're still standing is because the High Commander would not allow me to beam into your private quarters and challenge you directly. But now the High Commander isn't here." A weapon forms in Bogdan's hand, and he points it straight at my face.

Automatically, my helmet forms to fully shield my face. The spines have grown on my armor so that I am a mirror image to Bogdan, a Tsenturion in full battle array.

"You threaten an unarmed soldier?" I raise my empty hands. As long as I'm in the brig, my nanotech is blocked from forming a weapon, and he knows it. He also can't attack me. The barrier would block his thrusts; it's solid on both sides. "How honorable. How brave."

Bogdan absorbs the blade back into his armor. "I don't need a weapon to destroy you. Face me, if you dare." He hits the panel on the side of my confinement.

And the barrier between us disappears.

* * *

MARTA

"HIGH COMMANDER, if I may, these are excellent points," Medik says in his grandfatherly tone. Gavrill looks at the Medik with an *'E tu, Brutus?'* expression. He looks like he's in pain.

"Arkdhem has proved himself unworthy of a Tribute. Not that Tributes are objects." The High Commander turns to Dawn pleadingly, reaching out to her. "Dawn, I did not mean that you are an object or a reward. I understand that Tributes are people who should not be given out like trophies for good service."

"Do you?" Dawn huffs. "Because it sounds like you're trying to recall Marta like she's a toy Arkdhem can no longer play with."

"My love, no." The High Commander succeeds in capturing Dawn's hand. She begrudgingly lets him, her face averted. He's winning her back over. I bite my lip because I don't really want to break up their relationship too, any more than I want my own broken. "Tributes are a gift. But not because they are objects. Because your love is the most important thing, and shouldn't be squandered on the unworthy."

"You don't have to be worthy to receive unconditional love, that's the point," Dawn says, shaking her head. "You don't get to choose who the Tributes love."

"I will forever be grateful that you have given me yours." Gavrill kisses Dawn's knuckles. The moment is so tender, I avert my eyes. This smacks of an old argument.

"What Dawn is trying to say is that if you truly believe Tributes are equal to Tsenturions, you must afford them the same agency as you do yourself," Pareena is in counselor mode. "If there is to be any unbonding, it must be Marta's choice."

Still holding Dawn's hand, the High Commander shakes his head. There is now real pain on his face. If it wasn't my own future he was pained over, I might feel sorry for him. As it is, I'm okay with watching him wriggle like a worm on a hook for a while longer.

"I cannot allow a warrior who's abandoned his post to retain his Tribute. The punishment must fit the crime."

"With all due respect," Medik adds, "we are no longer simply a military society. Tsenturions and Tributes now form a civilian society, as well, at the same time as we are at war. We must forge a new path for our protocols and customs. By our old ways, as a warrior, Arkdhem would have never mated while performing his duties. Trying to assign old protocols to our current situation, while not acknowledging the changes happening, will only lead to more inconsistencies and issues."

"Hear hear," I murmur as the High Commander groans. Dawn pats his shoulder sympathetically, but there's a smug expression on her face. I only know that if they try to take me from Arkdhem, I won't let it happen without a fight. "If you try to mate me with someone new, I'll bite his dick and his fucking *seela* off."

Ignoring the High Commander's horrified look, I glance back down at my tablet to check on Arkdhem, and gasp loudly.

"What is it?" Pareena asks.

"Arkdhem's gone." I hold up the tablet, shock and worry pounding through me. The space where he'd been confined is now empty. What happened to him? Where did he go? I try to reach for him through the bond, but all I feel is anger, which I'm pretty sure is my own, considering the current topic of discussion.

Before I can completely freak out, Gavrill takes the tablet from me and taps the screen, changing the angle of the cameras.

Arkdhem appears again—and he's grappling with the huge warrior in black armor. *Who is that?*

"Dammit, Bodgan," Pareena snaps, shocking us all. "Not again." She shoves out of her seat, and rushes from the room.

CHAPTER 12

M arta

SNATCHING the tablet from the High Commander's hands, I bolt after Pareena, my heart pounding in my chest. Arkdhem is fighting! And not only that, he's fighting Pareena's mate! What the hell is going on?

But deep in my heart, I know... Pareena's mate is likely as pissed as the High Commander, but that doesn't mean it's okay to hurt my mate, dammit! Stupid Neanderthal warrior mentality.

"Tributes," the High Command roars after us, his chair scraping the floor as he rises. "I command you to halt! If two warriors are fighting, you cannot engage—"

"Oh, leave them alone," Dawn snaps. "We are NOT done talking about this—" Her voice is cut off as the door slides shut. *You tell it to him, Dawn!* Maybe she'll pound the message into Gavrill's thick head. In the meantime, I hope Arkdhem's all right. If he kills Pareena's mate...

I follow Pareena through the twisting halls of the Tsenturion ship, moving as fast as I can to keep up with her.

"I can't believe this. I thought he was over it…" Pareena mutters, before her voice goes quiet enough that I can't hear what she's saying anymore.

I want to ask her what's going on but she dashes around a corner at full speed, and I skid a little as I try to follow.

I can tell we're getting close to where Arkdhem is because battle cries are ringing out, echoing down the hallway. Ahead, several Tsenturion soldiers are peering through a door.

"Why are you just standing there?" Pareena shouts at them. She hustles forward at double time and whisks around them before they realize she's there.

"Wait!" One of the waiting soldiers notices her but it's too late—I've already dashed past him and the other three Tsenturions to enter the room as well. They were too distracted by Pareena to notice me until it was too late.

Just inside the door, Pareena stops short, and I crash into her. I don't blame her for stopping. The entire brig has turned into a battle scene.

Arkdhem and another warrior in black armor with fearsome spikes protruding from his helmet and back are going at it. The black-armored warrior is bigger and bulkier, but Arkdhem is taller and leaner, and that makes him more agile. The two of them are slugging it out with their fists, the snarls and roars terrifying to hear.

"Stop," Pareena yells at the same time as I shout Arkdhem's name. Neither of the warriors hears us. Pareena turns to one of the waiting Tsenturions, putting her hands on her hips. "Weren't your orders to guard the prisoner?"

"Yes?" one of the soldiers replies, and winces as Bogdan slams Arkdhem into the wall, shaking the entire room. I wince as well, watching them with my heart in my throat, but I know better than to step in. I don't want to give Bogdan ammunition against Arkdhem. He probably wouldn't hurt a Tribute on purpose, but I am Arkdhem's tribute, so maybe he wouldn't care. "But Commander Bogdan gave us orders—"

"So? You were supposed to be guarding Arkdhem *from* him. When your commander gives you a stupid order, don't indulge his idiocy!" Pareena yells at them. They all look at each other, unsure what to do.

"Oh my god," I mutter.

"Don't just stand there!" Pareena waves her arms at the guards. "Do something!"

The four soldiers look at each other as if waiting for the others to go first.

"Ah, well, Commander Bogdan told us to stay back and not interfere. We weren't actually told we were guarding Arkdhem from the commander, and we can't disobey a direct order—"

Pareena draws herself up to her full height, which is about half the size of the shortest Tsenturion, her eyes flashing. "*High* Commander Gavrill is on his way," she announces. "What will he say when he finds that you have allowed this fight to go on?"

The four warriors sigh. One by one, they shrug and their armor grows bulkier, their helmets forming to cover their faces.

"Stand back, Tributes," one of them orders, and the four of them wade into the fray.

"Well done," I whisper to Pareena.

"Thanks. Mentioning the High Commander usually works," she whispers back, rubbing her face with her hand. "We really do need to establish some new protocols though. The way the warriors follow orders can be good in some situations, but obviously it's not going to work all the time."

"I think they're more afraid of you than the High

Commander," I murmur. We share a brief smile, but then turn back to the fight, biting our lips.

The brig guards trudge over to the fighting warriors.

One of them raises his hand. "By order of the High Commander, we command you to stop—"

Before he can finish, Bogdan's fist smashes the warrior in the chest, sending him flying into the wall.

Pareena and I wince in unison.

Arkdhem kicks a guard down, and leaps over him to tackle the third. Bogdan jumps on the fourth. Both Arkdhem and Bogdan's arms rise and fall in synchronized punches. Guards One and Three fall to the ground. Great. Apparently, *now* they're going to get along and fight alongside each other instead of fighting each other.

Ugh. Men.

But it is a really impressive display of martial prowess. Pareena and I are suddenly getting a first-hand exhibition of why Bogdan and Arkdhem are the second- and third-in-command of the Tsenturions. When they were fighting each other, they'd been evenly matched—but fighting against two to one odds with other warriors?

Not a problem.

And it's not that the guards aren't highly skilled and vicious fighters themselves. They are, and I can tell, their movements happening in a blur, determination on their faces.

It's just that Arkdhem and Bogdan are that much better.

The second guard tries a sneak attack on Arkdhem from behind, lunging forward to wrap his arms around Arkdhem's shoulders. Without even pausing, Arkdhem snaps forward, using the guard's momentum to whirl and knock out Guard One, who had just staggered to his feet, with a roundhouse kick.

"Holy shit! KO!" I shout. Then I catch Pareena's eye and

grimace, falling back. "Sorry. Got caught up in the excitement." Is it my fault I had a thing for watching MMA and cage fights back home, and I forgot for a moment that there were serious stakes here?

She shakes her head and grumbles something about an overdose of testosterone being contagious around here. I bite my lip.

Guard Four has somehow grown what looks like a mace out of his armor. Pareena gasps as he swings it towards her mate's face. But spikes grow out of Bogdan's gauntlets, and *he catches the mace in his hands.* He doesn't even pause, pulling the guard towards him as he jerks his own knee up. The guard is bent over double when Bogdan slams him into the wall, and he topples down.

"Good job, babe!" Pareena cries, clapping her hands.

It's my turn to raise a brow in her direction. She covers her flushed cheeks and mumbles, "I guess it's easier to get carried away than I realized."

The brig guards are officially out of the fight. Three of them lie motionless by the wall. The other is groaning, his helmet half hanging off of his head.

But that means Arkdhem and Bogdan are free to attack each other again. And they waste no time trying to kick each other's ass.

Arkdhem leaps past Bogdan, smashing his helmet. One of Bogdan's spikes falls off.

But Bogdan turns and throws the mace at Arkdhem, catching my mate off guard.

Arkdhem staggers. Bogdan bellows in triumph, and gives chase.

"What do we do?" I cry.

Pareena shrugs helplessly, turning her attention back to her mate, fear and worry clear in her expression.

Now the two alien warriors have lost their weapons and

are grappling with each other. Bogdan punches Arkdhem's shoulder. Arkdhem shudders, his suit blackening with the blow, but remains upright to retaliate with an elbow to Bogdan's face.

Pareena and I are both holding our breath. At some point, we started holding hands.

I turn back to the fight. The force of the blows have torn some of the armor. There are small and large pieces of it littered around the room. A bigger piece—a breast or back-plate—lies in the middle, threatening to trip someone. I didn't realize the nanotech could come off that way.

Sections of Bogdan's and Arkdhem's armor have turned gray. Most of the spikes have broken off. It doesn't look good.

"They're going to fight until one surrenders." Or worse—someone gets fatally injured or dies.

I don't want that to happen to either of our mates.

After a few tense moments of grappling, Arkdhem slides out from Bogdan's grip and throws a punch that sends the larger warrior crashing down to the floor. On the way, Bogdan's leg flies out and manages to trip Arkdhem. The larger warrior finds his feet quickly while Arkdhem is still rolling away. In a lightning fast move, Bodgan is on him, fist rising high in the air. He's going to bash Arkdhem's skull in.

I don't even think. With a sharp cry—"No!"—I throw myself between Bogdan and Arkdhem, covering Arkdhem's head with my body.

"Marta!" Pareena's cry follows me. Bogdan cries out as well, I can hear the horror in his voice, but I can also feel his movement.

They're so fast, by the time I had thrown myself between them, his fist was already falling.

I'm braced, waiting for the inevitable pain, for my possible death. I have no armor. No protection. I've only known Arkdhem for a week. But it's in that moment that I also know, I've somehow fallen in love with him, and I would be willing to die for him. I have no regrets.

There's an explosion of sound next to my head, the screech of metal against metal, and I lift my head in a daze. Somehow, Bogdan managed to redirect his fist and it's slammed into the floor beside my shoulder, rather than actually hitting me.

The big male jerks back, up onto his feet, leaving me lying across Arkdhem's head. He stares at me and the indent he left in the ship's floor, as if realizing how close he came to killing me. I stare back at him, my heart pounding so fast that my chest feels tight, like it's closing in around itself, and I can barely breathe.

Pareena careens past us, slamming into her mate's chest, and wrapping her arms around him. The only way he and Arkdhem could get to each other now would be through the two of us.

"Enough," she tells him firmly.

Strong hands pick me up as Arkdhem pulls me off of his head, giving himself enough room to sit up. His golden face seems a little paler than normal, but otherwise unharmed as the nanotech peels back, exposing his skin.

"Are you okay?" I ask him, cupping his cheeks.

"Yes, my Marta." He stares at me like he's drinking me in with his eyes, trying to memorize every tiny millimeter of my face. Like he's afraid I'm going to be taken away from him again. I throw my arms around him, clinging to him. Fuck that. If they try to separate us again, they're going to have to deal with a hella pissed off Brazilian, and there's no way they're ready for that.

"What were you thinking?" Bogdan roars at Pareena.

"I was trying to knock some sense into you," she shouts right back. There's no sign of calm counselor Pareena. She pushes her long black hair out of her face, demon flames dancing in her eyes. "And I can ask you the same question. What were *you* thinking, attacking a fellow Tsenturion?" She pounds her tiny fist against his huge shoulder.

Before Bogdan can answer, the High Commander strides into the room, obviously seething. I don't need to see the colors of his armor to know that he's on the last leg of his patience.

Dawn's right behind him. She see us, gasps, and starts forward but he catches her and cradles her in front of him, his hands on her rounded belly.

Arkdhem scrambles to his feet, lifting me with him. We face the High Commander and Dawn in much the same position—me in front of Arkdhem with my back to his front and his arms around me. Beside us, Bogdan gently turns Pareena to mirror us, but not before she punches her mate's arm once more. I cross my arms over my chest and glare right back at the High Commander.

The brig guards have made it over to the door, and are helping each other up.

"I ordered you to watch the prisoner," the High Commander snaps at them. "What happened?"

The brig guards look at each other and then at Bogdan, silent and unsure of themselves.

"High Commander... Commander Bogdan ordered us to stand back and allow him to talk to Commander Ark—I mean, the prisoner." Guard One looks pained at having to narc on Bogdan, but he's also not going to lie to the High Commander. More cracks in their current protocols showing through. I can't help but feel a little smug. I'm going to shove all these cracks in the High Commander's face until he caves and gives me what I want—my mate.

"I goaded Bogdan to challenge and attack me," Arkdhem says smoothly.

"He is a traitor to our kind," Bogdan mutters.

The High Commander puts up one hand to stop them, glaring. "Enough. Report to the med bay," he orders the guards. They salute stiffly, and stagger off.

"And you two. What am I going to do with you? I should throw you *both* in the brig." The High Commander glares at them. "Bad enough that you have to go at each other, but you injured more warriors in your feud now! And endangered your Tributes!"

* * *

Arkdhem

STIFFENING, I hold more tightly to Marta than before. I had not known she was in danger. I wouldn't have expected her to be anywhere near me when Bogdan and I were fighting.

When she'd thrown herself atop me, in between Bogdan and myself, my entire world had come to a horrifying halt. I still couldn't believe she'd interfered in a Tsenturion duel and come out unharmed. For that, I owed Bogdan thanks for his superior self-control. She should have been killed, and I know it.

The need for gratitude rankles.

"Perhaps we should have a cooling down period," Pareena suggests in her more normal, calm voice. She squirms in Bogdan's arms as he fusses with her hair, already looking calmer now that she is with him.

"Maybe Arkdhem could just be confined to his quarters until the trial," Dawn suggests with a glance at me and Marta. I appreciate the gesture, but I already know that will not be granted. The Tributes have a great amount of sway in what happens to them. Not so much in what happens outside of their sphere.

But the High Commander shocks me.

"Very well," he says, though he does not look happy about it. Both Bogdan and I stare at him in shock. "Arkdhem, until the trial, you are to remain in your quarters, including for mealtimes. Your Tribute may come and go as she pleases."

I gape at him as Bogdan makes a disbelieving noise.

"You're just going to reward him with a vacation for committing treason?" He sounds enraged. I can't blame him. I expected to remain here for the rest of my time until my trial. And then to suffer far worse afterwards.

"Being stripped of command isn't a reward, just as being confined to quarters isn't a vacation," Gavrill growls back.

That is true. Knowing I am being stripped of my command is shameful. Everyone will know, and they will know why. But the why—Marta—makes it worth it.

"What about his Tribute?" Bogdan waves a hand towards us before securing it right back around his own Tribute. I snarl at him.

"Marta," my Tribute snaps, and I tighten my arms around her. I do not want Bogdan's attention drawn to her, but that does not stop her. "My name is Marta."

"Marta," the High Commander emphasizes her name, "will decide where she wishes to be."

There's something in the tone of his voice, in his expression, and I narrow my eyes at him, glancing at Dawn and Pareena. Both of them look pleased, and Dawn actually pats his arm.

Ah, the Tributes at work again. They have changed us so much, from Dawn's arrival, and then more changes wrought after Pareena's. But I have no complaints.

"I want to stay with Arkdhem," Marta says.

Happiness surges through me so strongly that I could

explode with it. It's easy to ignore the sound Bogdan makes. My Tribute, my Marta, just chose to stay with me. There is no better feeling in all the universe.

The High Commander nods. He doesn't look particularly happy either, but he does not tell Marta she cannot or that she should not. Yes, I certainly detect the deft hands of our Tributes in the High Commander's change of heart.

"Very well. At any point, if you wish to leave, you have only to comm the bridge."

"I can do that," Marta says. She rubs her forehead and I sense relief coursing through her. I cuddle her closer.

"Bogdan, you clearly incited this incident," the High Commander continues. "For that, I am going to transfer your command from the bridge—for the next two cycles—to overseeing the waste compaction on level eighteen."

Trash duty. Another time I would have enjoyed his punishment far more, but being entirely stripped of my rank is far worse.

"But—" Bogdan protests.

"Argue with me, and I'll add another few semicycles of assisting Medik in the med bay. You can clean and sanitize all the fluid sample containers."

"So I get trash duty, and he gets a free vacation with his Tribute," Bogdan grumbles.

"Yes," the High Commander replies seriously. "And it's your fault. If you hadn't attacked him, he would still be residing in the brig."

This time, I do have to bite back my smile. I am free, and it is Bogdan's fault.

"Don't forget, he's been stripped of his command," Gavrill adds. "Your trash duty is temporary. His punishment might be permanent."

Bogdan shuts up, and lets Pareena lead him away.

But Gavrill's grim pronouncement has wiped my good

LEE SAVINO & GOLDEN ANGEL

humor away. Is that a hint at what's to come? A permanent demotion? Will I be cast down to the bottom ranks of warriors, to work myself back up again?

There is no shame at being in the bottom rank, but there is in losing rank. It is a grave dishonor.

Marta makes a noise of concern, and I push my regrets away. Whatever shame I must bear, whatever punishment I must endure, she is worth it. I said it before, and I meant it.

"We will escort you to your quarters," the High Commander says, and I nod. Gesturing, he steps aside and I reluctantly let go of Marta so she can move. She immediately grabs onto my hand—which pleases me—and the four of us walk down the hall.

CHAPTER 13

M *arta*

"Do you need medical attention?" the High Commander asks, eying Arkdhem as he and Dawn escort us through the hallway. Dawn seems mollified when it comes to the High Commander, but I'm not feeling quite so generous.

While I'm getting some of what I want, it's hard to forget that he's still going to be the one in charge of disciplining my mate. I'll trust that he'll let us remain together after Arkdhem's trial is over. Until then, I remain wary.

"No." Arkdhem shrugs his shoulder and winces. The nanotech there is still grey. He and Bogdan really beat the hell out of each other. I want to smack him and hug him at the same time. "I have a basic armor repair kit in my quarters. And a rest cycle will fix most of the damage."

For a moment, I think the High Commander is going to say something, but instead he sighs. I sneak a glance at him and there's a faraway expression in his eyes, like he's thinking.

We walk in silence the rest of the way, which is a little uncomfortable, but I don't feel up to breaking it. When we've reached Arkdhem's quarters, the High Commander blocks the door to face us.

"I have not forgiven you for what you've done," he says to Arkdhem. "By leaving your command when we were planet side, you left us exposed. All turned out well, but that does not negate the risk or the choice you made by not contacting me. The chain of command exists for a reason, and that does not change even though we now have Tributes."

Dawn looks troubled, maybe because it's impossible to argue that point. She bites her lip, and I look down. My mind races, but I can't come up with a good point against what the High Commander said, other than I'm glad Arkdhem came for me. But would I have still been glad if it *had* meant harm to others?

No. No, I would not have been.

"I understand," Arkdhem says quietly. "I cannot apologize for retrieving my Marta, but I wish I had contacted you before leaving." That's the first time he's said so, but I think he means it. Seeing the High Commander's reactions, maybe Arkdhem now realizes the High Commander wouldn't have left him hanging.

The High Commander nods, his expression grave.

"You will suffer the consequences. The Council will meet in three daycycles. Until then, you remain here with your Tribute." Stepping aside, he gestures. Dawn is clinging to his arm and she gives me a look as Arkdhem opens the doors to his quarters and we step inside, as if to say that she'll do what she can.

I hope she can do a lot, because the High Commander's final words to us don't do much for my confidence.

"She is the only reason I haven't forcibly broken your bond. She spoke up for you. You owe her a debt."

I'm holding my breath. My body's shaking with the aftermath of everything. The thought our bond breaking makes my legs wobble like I might collapse.

I didn't even know I had a bond, but I don't want to lose it.

What if the Council decides to split us up anyway? How much power does the High Commander have?

My fear must show on my face because Dawn gives me a quiet thumbs up. But she drops her hand before her mate turns to her.

And with that, the doors to Arkdhem's quarters glide shut.

The second the door slides shut, Arkdhem swings me towards him and brings his mouth to mine. He cradles the back of my head gently but his lips are not so gentle on mine, his tongue thrusting, plundering. I lean back and hug my arms around his neck, pulling him towards me.

He lifts me up without taking his mouth from mine, and walks to the bed. I end up on his lap. We make out like high schoolers at a drive-in theater.

Then he's grabbing the back of my neck and turning me, guiding me belly down over his lap.

"What's going on? I squeak. I wriggle but get nowhere. Arkdhem's pulling up my robe thingy and no sooner than my upturned bottom is bare is his hand crashing down.

Crack!

"If you ever put yourself in danger like that again..." The fear in his tone alarms me more than anything.

"I won't. I promise." I kick. "I'm sorry... I wouldn't have done it. I thought you were going to die!"

He wrenches me upwards and fastens his mouth to mine again, kissing me like it's the last thing he'll do. I hold onto his shoulders and accept his kiss, hoping to calm his fears.

He pulls back, his chest heaving. His eyes close a moment. "When I saw the weapon leave Bogdan's hands, and I was across the room and I could do nothing to help you…"

"I didn't know what else to do. It was not my finest moment. I won't do it again." I place my hands on either side of his face until he looks at me. "But how can you ask me to remain on the sidelines when your life is threatened?"

"I do not deserve you," he breathes.

I surge up in his arms to meet his mouth, and for a long while we swap bites and licks and half kisses, drinking of each other until I'm drunk on him and woozy.

When he finally fists his fingers in my hair and draws back my head, the slight bite of pain is delicious and brings me back.

"You put your life in danger," he growls, his hand tightening in my hair, enough to sting. It's also hot as hell, and a little scary because my butt is suddenly tingling, as if in warning of what's to come. Naughty girls get punished.

My half closed eyes fly open.

"Never come between two fighting warriors," he says, giving me a little shake.

"It was dumb, I know," I confess, which isn't going to help my case any.

Arkdhem's eyes slit, but his grip loosens on my hair. "My heart almost left my body." His hands slide to cup my face. "You are my heart, Marta. You must take greater care." His thumb rubs my bottom lip. "It gives me no pleasure to tell you, you have earned a punishment."

I almost snort. He's not displeased about having to punish me. His cock is rock hard under my butt.

I'm tempted to echo what he's been telling Gavrill and say

something like 'I accept the consequences,' but school my face into a serious mask.

He feathers another kiss on my lips before lifting me up and undressing me slowly. The garments slip away easily. Maybe that's what's up with these Tribute robe things— they're designed to be removed quickly.

When the fabric is pooled at my feet, he orders me to go to the bed. "All fours, now."

Heart pounding, I do what he commands. My pussy is already wet. It seems to be excited at the thought of punishment, knowing how that's been twined with erotic pleasure in the past.

As if sensing the turn of my thoughts, Arkdhem adds, "You are not to come."

Damn, of course not. This is punishment.

I peek behind me. Arkdhem's gone to the replicator and gotten a cane. He snaps it against his leg. It whistles through the air and leaves a long gray line on his armor.

I suck in a breath. That's going to hurt.

I quickly turn back before he notices me peeking. If he does catch me, he doesn't say anything. He returns to my side and sets a hand in my back.

"Three with the cane," he says simply. I try not to whimper.

The strikes come quick as lightning.

Slash! Slash! Two horizontal burning lines cross my backside. The third and final one is angled across the other two.

Backside smarting, I wait to see what else will happen. Three cane strikes, harsh as they are, can't be the whole of my punishment.

I don't have long to wait. The Bride Trainer starts stretching and filling my ass, as per usual. This time, the plug grows to a greater thickness. It's uncomfortable as hell, but my pussy is still dripping.

Arkdhem strokes my bottom. The plug fills me to the point where I want to moan. If Arkdhem pulled it out after a few minutes, my asshole would be gaping. Does that mean he's finally going to...

"Naughty tributes get their asses fucked," he says. "And they don't get to come."

I shiver. My nipples are hard points. This is going to be a really enjoyable punishment—for him. Suddenly, there's a little extra burn inside my stretched rear.

"While I'm waiting for you to be ready, I think I'll warm your bottom, inside and out."

The plug is really burning now, and I'm squirming. What has he done?

"I believe the manuals call this 'figging.' It's an ancient technique usually involving ginger." Arkdhem rubs my bottom, the soothing touch counterpoint to the teeth-gritting sting within. "I was able to replicate it quite nicely."

"It hurts," I whine.

"It's supposed to." He checks my pussy, his long finger gliding and hooking around to massage the inner wall until a lovely warmth spreads through me. "And yet... you're wet." I can hear his smirk.

Damn him. He knows how much I respond to these punishments.

The burn in my bottom is getting worse.

Arkdhem has me kneel up and box my arms behind my back so he can play with my breasts, caressing them, pinching my nipples, watching my expression carefully.

I'm almost grateful when he plucks at my nipples because the sensation dulls the sting in my backside a little.

"Shall I do something to help with the pain?" he asks.

I narrow my eyes at him. It sounds like a trick question. "Whatever you like, Master," I answer carefully.

He grins and tips me over his lap, propping my ass high in

the air. Now his big palm is swatting my already cane-striped ass. He'll turn it pink between the red lines.

He smacks each cheek, dividing it into four quadrants again—six including my sit-spots. He peppers each quadrant. The sharp sensation of his palm distracts a little from the cruel bite of the ginger-like plug, but when he stops, my bottom is throbbing—inside and out.

"Ow, ow, ow," I chant. Did I ever wonder what figging would feel like? I wish I could go back in time and delete that particular fantasy. This sucks.

The skin around the plug feels seared. The plug is still growing, stretching me even wider.

Suddenly, Arkdhem spanks the plug.

I gasp but my pussy juices further. He spanks it again and then suddenly the plug begins to vibrate.

"Oh no..." I writhe on his hard lap.

"Yes." His fingers rub my pussy folds, collecting moisture. He presents his fingers to my lips, making me taste my own juices.

Then he eases me off his lap and down to my knees before him. He pulls my head up to face the broad head of his cock. The *seela* suckers latch on to my face.

I'll definitely have face hickies after this. And if any of the Tributes see me, they'll know exactly what happened. Heat floods my face at the thought.

Arkdhem makes me suck him, holding my hair and guiding my head. The cane gives me a warning tap from time to time, threatening to swat my ass when I don't follow instructions quite right. I bob my head vigorously, trying to win his favor as my ass burns. Arkdhem grunts above me, his cock seeming to swell in my mouth. I redouble my efforts. Maybe if I please him enough, he'll let me have a turn... which I need desperately. Even though my ass is on fire, I have never been so turned on.

But he pulls out of my mouth suddenly. The *seela* come off my cheeks with little pops. He tugs my hair, moving me into a new position. I rise off my knees and scramble to follow his lead. I end up on the bed, propped on my hands and knees. The cane taps the insides of my thighs, forcing me to spread them wide.

Arkdhem places the cane in my line of sight, and presses on my back until my face is planted into the bed, cheek to the coverlet. My ass is high in the air. Presented to him.

My thighs quiver with the strain of keeping my legs so wide, but my nipples are hardened points pressing into the bed. Arkdhem cups my ass and all my attention goes to the mass of sensation in my bottom.

The Bride Trainer melts away, leaving my ass gaping wide, but empty. The burn is gone and I melt in relief, but then the broad head of Arkdhem's cock breaches my entrance. It stings, burns, aches…

He moves slowly, letting me feel every inch of his cock as it pushes into my ass. I moan, shuddering, clenching. Would a human cock feel different? I'll never know. The sensations are odd, but I don't know if it's only because he's an alien, or because he's in my ass.

It hurts, and yet it feels good. It stings, and yet it throbs. I pant for breath as he fills me, feeling as though there's not enough room in my body for all the air I need. I can't draw a deep breath, not while he's still sliding into me, invading my most intimate space and claiming me completely.

I whimper as he bottoms out, his *seela* stroking the curves of my ass. I feel his cock flexing inside me, the strange head moving and massaging my inner walls. It's depraved torment, the kind that messes with my head as much as my body.

I've never let a man take me like this. Never would have, back on Earth. I wasn't saving it, exactly, I just never thought

I'd want anyone to do this to me. Not that Arkdhem asked. And that makes me even hotter, even though back on Earth I'd cut off a man's balls for the presumption.

But he's not a man. He's Arkdhem. My warrior. My mate. My everything, whether I ever admit it aloud or not.

"You will not come," he orders, but then he drops his hand, reaching around my hip to massage my pussy.

Not fair!

Pleasure sparks through me. I grit my teeth and try to focus on the burning stretch in my ass.

"Arkdhem—" I gasp. "Master, please."

He smacks my labia lightly. "No."

The sharp swat makes me grit my teeth but at least it made my orgasm fade. Except, it didn't, not really. The mess of sensations—the stretch, the burn, the fullness, the slight cramping in response to Arkdhem's huge rod filling my back channel, the tension in my back and the delicate little nibbles of the *seela* on my chastised bottom—it all swirls into a whirlpool of overwhelming feeling. And even though most of those sensations should not be pleasurable, they add to the growing pressure of my orgasm.

"Master," I half-whine, half-beg.

"This is punishment, my heart." But he takes his hand away and grips the front of my thigh, pulling me more fully against him. "Now, attend to my pleasure."

His arrogant order sends shivers of delight through me. But I'm not sure how I can do anything, stretched and stuffed and half mindless from fighting my climax.

I can only grip the sheets and hold on as his thrusts rock me forward into the bed.

* * *

Arkdhem

137

. . .

My Tribute's ass is impossibly tight and burning hot. I'm fighting my own climax as I glide in and out of her tight channel. Her flesh is rosy from my palm. Her bottom clenches on my cock, the ring of muscle tightening around my member. My *seela* aid my thrusts, suctioning greedily to her chastised flesh.

Through the bond, Marta's emotions wash through me. She's overwhelmed by sensation, vacillating between the forces of pleasurable pain and painful pleasure.

Moving harder, faster, I let my emotions take the reins of my movements, pounding into Marta's rear entrance with all my frustration, all my fear.

The manuals referred to this joining as 'naughty girl sex,' and I completely understand as I fill her forbidden hole. The taboo adds to the excitement, and I can feel it in the fluttering of her pulse and her emotions.

To take her in this manner does not provide pure pleasure. There is pain as well, despite the care I took in breaching her, and yet she bears it for me. For my pleasure.

I have never experienced the like. It's not just her willing submission, it's what she's willing to do for me. How far she's willing to go. For me. Singly. For so long, the Tsenturion race has been about what is good for the whole of us, but she saw me. Arkdhem.

She chose me.

Insisted on staying with me.

Let me claim her, fully, in the manner of her people, enduring pain for me, giving her pleasure over to me.

I grip her hips harder, pounding into her from behind. With each thrust, my *seela* pop off and fasten back on, and she cries out as they ignite more sparks of pain from my spanked behind. I can feel the heat emanating from the welts through the sensitive organs, and they stroke along her raised flesh, my fascination echoed by my body's response.

"Oh god," Marta gasps, writhing and bucking beneath me. I can feel her muscles clenching around me, increasing my own pleasure. I can hear the confusion in her voice, feel it in my core, as she is caught between pain and pleasure. "Please, Master. I'm going to come."

"Naughty Tribute," I murmur, watching my *seela* stroke along her bottom, my fingers digging into her hips as pleasure wracks me as well. "Very well. If you can come while I fuck your ass, you may."

I will not deny her ecstasy if she manages it. She has earned it.

I thrust hard, pounding into her from behind, reveling in the way she cries out, her scream rising higher and higher until she goes wild beneath me. I bury myself inside her, groaning with my own climax as she squeezes my cock, milking my orgasm from me in long, rapturous spurts. I can feel her coming around me, as lost to the pleasure as I am, my own echoing back at her and sending both of us careening through sheer sexual bliss as the connection between us enhances every bit of our mutual pleasure.

When she goes limp beneath me, I panic for a moment before realizing she is merely unconscious. Blissed out. Such things were spoken of in the manuals.

It is with smug satisfaction that I clean her and myself up. When I curl my body around hers, I feel her stirring again, and she moans a little.

Kissing the top of her head, I pull her in closer to me.

"Holy fuck… I am wrecked…"

I don't understand what she is saying, but 'wrecked' does not usually mean anything good.

"You are perfect," I respond, stroking my fingers through her hair.

"Right back at ya." She yawns. Her tone is flippant, but I can feel the depth of her emotion radiating through the bond, because my own matches hers, and the two amplify each other.

Still, I keep things light, sensing her desire for levity after such an intimate experience.

"Whenever you disobey me, you will get the naughty girl sex," I tell her, still stroking her hair. She wriggles against me, making a small humming noise. Still, she should know there are real consequences. "You are never to put yourself in danger again. I will not be so gentle for a second infraction."

"I won't," she mumbles, half asleep and fading fast.

My arms tighten around her, my voice lowering to a whisper. I'm not even sure she can hear me, but in some ways, that makes the words easier to say.

"I cannot live without you. You are my heart."

CHAPTER 14

WHEN SLEEP PEELS AWAY SLOWLY, the first thing I feel is my sore bottom. It feels hot as a dying sun. No wonder I ended up sleeping on my stomach. I touch my cheeks, half expecting raised marks from the *seela* suckers. My skin is smooth, but my lips are tender and puffy from the plundering kisses.

I roll to my side, stretching from the awkward position. A shadow falls over me—it's Arkdhem, holding a glass of water.

"I thought you might be thirsty," he murmurs. I reach for the glass greedily. The movement tips me to my back and I yelp. Planting my feet on the bed, I raise my hips up so my poor throbbing bottom is elevated.

"Let me help you." Arkdhem sounds faintly amused. He shifts me into his lap, letting me lean against him so my weight is centered on my hip. I gulp the entire glass in one go as he holds me. He strokes back my sleep-tousled hair and, when I'm done drinking, moves onto tracing my eyebrows and my kiss-swollen lips. I close my eyes and let him retrace the marks he's left on my body.

I want to wake up slowly, savor this moment. It so easily could have been different.

"We came close to being separated, didn't we?" I ask.

"Yes, my heart." He runs a finger down the line of my jaw, pausing to press on a few tender spots. Maybe I do have some face hickeys.

I catch his fingers and meet his gaze. "I won't let it happen. I'll fight for you."

He squeezes my hand. "I don't deserve you."

"Perhaps not." I shift on his lap, wincing when my bottom comes in contact with his hard thighs. But I want this conversation to happen face to face. "I want to be with you, Arkdhem. I know we've just met, but this…" I lick my lips, searching for words. It's time to be honest. To dissolve any boundaries between us. I've never lowered my walls for someone like this. It's scary, but exhilarating. "They asked me if we had a bond. I said yes."

Arkdhem turns his head and kisses my fingers. "I feel it too," he murmurs.

"For this to work, we need to be honest. I don't want anything between us."

"I understand."

"So why did you do it? Why did you disobey orders if you knew the consequences? Help me understand." The questions that have been bubbling in my mind are coming up to the surface again, but more than that, I want to help him form his defense for the trial. There has to be something we can use to gain him leniency.

His eyes unfocus, like he's seeing something I cannot.

"The Jabol are our allies… but recently, the High Commander was given cause to mistrust them. The Vgotha, whom we blamed for the destruction of Tsentur, used Pareena and Dawn to gain an audience with the High Commander."

My lips press shut from asking questions. There's something in his voice, or maybe it's the bond that I feel, that makes me think he doesn't really want to talk about this. That he's not sure he believes it. I don't want to distract him or pull him off topic. I'm also having trouble reconciling Frllil and the Jabol with the picture I was getting from the other Tsenturions.

"They claimed that long ago, the Vgotha were captives of the Jabol. Forced to work in the mines and do physical labor to support the Jabol society."

"They were slaves," I say flatly when he pauses. Thankfully, that's all he needs to prod him back into talking.

"Yes. And then their leader Tor found a way to free them. The Vgotha claim they simply wanted freedom and a place to live in peace. But the Jabol wanted to keep them enslaved. Many Vgotha were killed, and they retaliated... and then the Jabol decided they needed help. Firepower. Warriors. The Jabol say that the Vgotha destroyed our planet, and we trusted them. They had been longtime traders with us. We had never heard of the Vgotha before, but after meeting them in battle multiple times, it was easy to believe what the Jabol said of them."

He rubs his chin and I bite my lip, sensing he's going to say more. Waiting for it.

"The Vgotha showed us a vid of the Jabol destroying our planet. Some kind of weapons that rained down destruction on our people. The only reason our fleet survived was because our ships were in deep space on an exploratory mission. When we returned, there was nothing left of our home but rubble. The planet and everyone on it was gone."

I'd read about some of it in Frllil's files, blaming the

destruction on the Vgotha, but that didn't have the same kind of emotional impact as talking to someone who was actually affected by it. Who had returned to his planet to find it gone. His family and friends, gone. The only ones left being those who were with him.

"That's awful," I whisper. *Fuck Frllil, too, if he knew about all this and didn't tell me. But would he have? He seemed so dedicated to the program, to continuing the Tsenturions' race... is that motivated by guilt, though?* "I'm so, so sorry."

"It was a long time ago, my heart."

A long time ago, but I can feel the echo of my own sadness inside me, a deep, empty ache that throbs and pulses like a physical node in the center of my chest. He's not over it. How could he be?

"So that's why you didn't want to leave me with the Jabol." I press my fingers to my chest where I can feel his pain, thinking fast.

All the conversations I've heard finally make more sense. I can tell Arkdhem is torn about whether or not to believe the Vgotha's version of events, but the High Commander and Bogdan apparently find them credible.

Because Pareena and Dawn were the ones to facilitate the communication?

I really need to talk to the other Tributes about this as soon as I get the chance.

"Is there any way the Vgotha's vid could have been faked?"

Would all this advanced alien tech make that easier, or more difficult? It's impossible for me to know.

"Perhaps. It would be difficult, but..." Arkdhem shrugs, appearing troubled. "The Vgotha say they received the vid from the Riknari."

"Who are they?" I was starting to feel a little exasperated, not to mention frustrated. No one had mentioned a fourth group!

* * *

Arkdhem

Blinking, I refocus on my mate, whose impatience is making itself known to me. I give myself a little shake, the corners of my lips curving upwards.

"You have fitted yourself so well into my life already, sometimes I forget that you have not always been here. I apologize. I do not mean to leave you in ignorance." The temper that was flashing in her eyes softens, and I pull her to me, giving her temple a kiss. "The Riknari are known throughout the universe for their dedication to both justice and peace. They help those who are unable to help themselves—such as, if the Vgotha were enslaved by the Jabol, the Riknari would want to help them."

Falling silent, I again ponder whether or not I truly believe the Vgotha were given their tech by the Riknari. If it is true...

"Have the Riknari ever been wrong?" Marta's face has that blank expression I have come to recognize from when she is processing information. It is another question that I did not expect, because none of us would ever think to ask such a thing.

"Not that I know of." I shake my head. "It's said they have an all-seeing oracle, who is able to see every side of a situation and come to a fair and just conclusion. I have never heard of an instance of the Riknari taking a side that was undeserving or which abused their trust."

Though, now, I do have to wonder. Could the Vgotha have fooled the Riknari somehow?

There are certain certainties that I have taken for granted for so long, it never occurred to me to question them. I know the High Commander puts great stock in the Vgotha's claim that the Riknari gifted them with the technology to defeat their oppressors.

But it also brings up the question: if the Riknari were aware of the situation with the Vgotha and the Jabol, if they knew about us and had the tape of Tsentur's destruction, why would they not have championed our cause? Offered their help to us?

I know the High Commander's point of view, which is that the Riknari are a small race and they could not be everywhere at once, but it still doesn't sit well with me. Why the Vgotha and not us? If they helped the Vgotha at all.

Marta's fingers caress my arm, settling some of the tension that has begun to grow in my body.

"And someone saying the 'oracle said' is enough proof for your High Commander?"

I do not blame her for the dubious quality to her question. It would not be enough for me, and I do not think it would be for the High Commander, not when coming from a source we have no reason to trust.

"No, the Vgotha said the Riknari provided the vid of Tsentur's destruction from the Jabol's own records."

I shake my head, as if doing so could clear away some of the images that flit through my mind. I will never forget watching that vid for as long as I live.

* * *

Marta

Arkdhem's mood has gone dark, not that I can blame him.

But... the Jabol's own records? The same ones Frllil gave me access to?

There's a spark in the back of my head, a blinking light in the darkness. The barest hint of a fairy light, tugging me onward. I used to feel this way when I stumbled onto something good—key information, a witness, or whistleblower willing to talk. My editor said I had a 'nose' for a good story. And now my writerly senses are tingling.

I keep real quiet. That's the first journalistic lesson I learned: once you're with a source, listening is ninety-nine percent of the job.

"And even though you weren't sure about the Jabol's guilt, you defied his orders and came for me anyway."

The monumental decision that changed his life, and not for the better. But he did it for me. If he hadn't, and the High Commander had decided against retrieving me, what would my fate have been? I shiver, because although I like to think that Frllil would have sent me back to Earth, I also don't know if it would have been possible. Were any of the enhancements he'd given me reversible? Would he have cared? Or would I have been written off as a regrettably failed experiment?

"I couldn't leave you with the Jabol for one microcycle longer than necessary. If there was a slight chance the Jabol had done this heinous thing, I didn't want you in their clutches. They might easily find out that the Tsenturions learned the truth, and hold you for ransom. Or... worse."

I bite my lip because Arkdhem's thoughts so closely align with mine. And he was assuming that the Tsenturions would have wanted me, would have cared what happened to me. I'm not so sure that's true.

Not fun to think about. I almost make a face. I'm glad Arkdhem didn't leave me there for long. I'm glad he's my mate. I squeeze his hand, and he returns the pressure.

There's a long silence. Arkdhem seems lost in thought. So I ask the question I know the tribunal will ask.

"Why did you go without notifying the High Commander?"

"Because I didn't want to risk him telling me not to go."

His brows form a surly line. "I broke the chain of command for you, Marta. And I'd do it again."

"Well, that's a lot." I joke, blinking a few times because my eyes are stinging. Not that I'm getting emotional or anything. There's a feeling in my chest, like some tightness has eased. My brain wants me to say something meaningful back to him—I feel like I should, but I have no idea what. I'm not good at this at all. I give him a subdued smile. "Thank you for telling me."

"Do you have any questions?"

"Not at this moment." I rub my face briskly, wiping away any trace of tears that might have leaked out. "I think I need to process everything, and then I'll have questions."

"I understand." He leans forward to kiss me softly on the forehead. "I must go to work now."

"I thought you weren't allowed to leave your quarters."

"I will work at my private station here. I must finish handing over my command."

My insides twist. This has to really suck for him, losing everything he's worked for. If it does, he hides it well. But then, he would, wouldn't he? He's the type who wouldn't want to make me feel bad. He might spank like a sadist, but deep down, he's a bit of a cinnamon roll.

But, of course, because I'm me, I have to keep pushing.

"How do you feel about that?"

He touches my hair. "You are worth any price."

More tightness in me unravels. I believe him. He's waited a long time for a mate. Maybe he won't blame and resent me, after all.

"I think I'm going to rest a little bit more." I shift onto the bed, and wince as my tender backside touches the sheets.

He looks smug. "When I return, I will bathe you. It will help you heal."

I nod and curl up on the bed. I close my eyes and wait

until he's left the room. I might have told him a little lie. I do want to rest, but I also want to talk to Frllil.

I still have the comm that will supposedly let me reach him, though I haven't tried to use it yet. With Arkdhem in the other room with the door shut, he shouldn't hear me.

For this story, I want to go straight to the source.

CHAPTER 15

I HUNCH down close to the bed until my mouth is only inches away from the pillow, which will hopefully muffle the sound.

I press my finger to my ear, hoping that it works as easily as Frllil said it would. I don't hear anything.

"Frllil," I whisper, trying to activate the comm in my ear. Does it need more than me pressing it? Silently, I curse myself for not asking more questions, but it's not like there had been time to.

When his voice comes on, it is a little crackly with static, but clear enough for me to easily make out his words. "Marta Romero Flores. I am here."

Despite all that Arkdhem's told me, I feel some relief when I hear Frllil's voice. He might be part of an alien species full of criminal masterminds, but I felt like we were friends. Ish. I think. Ugh, I hate having to second guess my gut—I've relied on my instincts for so long, it feels wrong to have to do so.

"I have some questions," I say and hesitate. I don't want to tell him everything Arkdhem told me, but on the other hand, I don't want anyone else caught up in this crazy mess. "Are there any more Tributes coming in?"

"I have not yet located the next match, no."

My gut says to trust Frllil. My brain is screaming against it. But if I'm going to, then now is the time. He doesn't have a new Tribute, so I don't have to worry about anything bad happening to another human woman if the Vgotha are telling the truth. And the priority is finding out who we can trust.

On the other hand, if it turns out I shouldn't trust Frllil, I don't want him to know that the Tsenturions and Vgotha are in contact with each other. Thankfully, there's a good reason why the Tsenturions might be questioning the Jabol that has nothing to do with the Vgotha.

"Have you heard of the Riknari?"

"Yes. What is the problem, Marta Romero Flores?" There's a touch of impatience in his voice, which prods at my temper. "I do not have time for these odd questions. I have my duties to fulfill."

Yeah, that's what worries me. I've met a lot of people willing to do monstrous things in the name of 'duty.' It's not hard to believe that there might be aliens willing to do the same. My own emotions are harder for me to control than usual. Because of Arkdhem's influence on me? Because of the bond?

I don't know, but I know it's partly my temper rising that prompts me to be blunter than usual.

"The Riknari have contacted the Tsenturions and told them the Jabol have a weapon that destroyed their planet."

"That would be unthinkable," Frllil says immediately, not

a hint of hesitation in his answer. "We are a peaceful race, dedicated to research."

How unthinkable is it really, though?

Because, the more I think about it, the more sense it makes. If they're such a peaceful race, having a warrior race at their beck and call would be good, right?

"The Riknari say the Vgotha were enslaved by the Jabol."

"They were not enslaved. We are technologically superior. We traded their services for our technology." He sounds like a small child, reciting a history lesson. But I'm from Earth and I know all too well how some people like to rewrite history, especially when it covers topics that make them or their ancestors look bad.

"What happened when they didn't want to make that trade anymore?" I ask.

"I... well, they left, of course. And then attacked us because they were angry that we did not want to give them our technology for free." He's so matter-of-fact about it, as if he's never questioned what he's been told once in his life.

"Have you ever looked into that?"

"What? No. Of course not. There is no reason to. The Illumination Guides would not lie to us. That would be unthinkable."

This is like dealing with a child. Maybe he's right to have blind faith in these leaders, but I've only ever seen blind faith go wrong. Maybe the aliens are more like humans than I thought, even the ones like the Jabol, who look and seem nothing like us.

Or maybe that's just my human cynicism. All I know is, I'm not willing to take Frllil's blind faith to my own heart. I have always questioned everything, and I'm much more into the Riknari way of trying to see things from all sides so I have all the information before I start making judgment calls. It's clear Frllil hasn't considered the Vgotha side of things at all, or questioned anything he's been told. Which I don't understand at all, but that's how it's sounding to me.

I blow out a breath, pressing my forehead against the pillow and closing my eyes. "Frllil, is it possible your Illumination Guides, if they had such a weapon, would annihilate the Tsenturion planet without telling the general populace?"

"Without a public debate? They are our guides, they do not make decisions for all of us without informing everyone. It would be unthinkable." He pauses as he says that word again, like he's realizing how many things he's saying are 'unthinkable,' and is finally thinking about them. I bite my lip to keep quiet and let him work through whatever he needs to mentally. When he speaks again, his voice is much more subdued. "They would not but... if they did then the record would be in the Archives. Everything must be Archived."

"Is there any chance I can look?"

"It is raw data. You cannot assimilate it. There is so much information in the Archives that we Jabol rarely attempt to assimilate all of it, we focus on our own areas of research." There's something in his voice now, like he's realizing that maybe he's taken a lot on faith without actually researching it. He sounds almost distracted. "I could look, though. If what you say is true..." His voice trails off. He still doesn't believe it. Doesn't want to believe it. I don't blame him. Sometimes ignorance truly is bliss, at least for the ignorant, especially when it allows them to ignore the harm they've done to others. He adds in a softer voice, "The Tsenturions might want revenge."

"We need to know the truth, Frllil," I say, coaxing him. "If you think you can do it without getting into trouble... Please. You must see how important this is."

If it's true, it means that not only have the Tsenturions been lied to, but it sounds like a large portion of the Jabol have, as well, about a lot of things.

"I will scour the Archives," Frllil says finally. "I will comm you once I know the truth. You will see. They could not have done this. It is unthinkable." His voice sounds like he's determined to prove me wrong, and I hope he's right. I really do.

"Thank you, my friend."

"Yes, Marta. I am your friend, and you are mine."

With that, the comm goes silent.

I drop onto my side, curl up, and close my eyes. I can rest now. Soon, I'll know the truth and I can share it with Arkdhem. It feels like a good thing.

Hours later, I am awoken when Arkdhem comes and carries me to the bath. I want to tell him about my research with Frllil, but bite my lip. Later. When I have answers.

The hot water makes me hiss. Arkdhem studies all my bruises.

"I should not have waited so long to apply the healing cream," he says, examining a particularly angry looking welt.

"It was meant to be punishment." I shrug. "I kind of like them." I go to straddle his lap and grit my teeth when the movement awakens new soreness. The soothing bath is helping, but not much.

He grimaces, shaking his head. "This is too much. I will take you to Medik."

"Oh my god." I cover my face with my hands. Medik is going to see evidence of our sexual perversion. Of course, he probably knows all about it; he probably was the one who gave the manuals to Arkdhem in the first place. "I'm seriously okay, I would tell you if I wasn't."

And to be honest, I'm going to be kind of pissed if I lose my bruises. They feel like badges of honor, not something that needs medical attention. My sadist cinnamon roll doesn't seem to know which of his instincts to lead with.

"Come, my Tribute." Arkdhem scoops me out of the

water. He wraps a towel around me but I'm still damp when he starts out the door.

"I can walk," I protest, clutching the towel over my breasts. "They're just bruises!

* * *

Arkdhem

SHAKING MY HEAD, I put Marta down on the bed as a chime at the door sounds. Marta jumps, apparently not having realized that I've already summoned Medik, that I did so when I was still looking her over.

"Enter."

"You could've let me get dressed," Marta grumbles, tightening the towel around herself. I give her a look of amusement as Medik enters. There is no reason to be shy in front of him.

"My Tribute may have suffered harm," I explain, getting up and gesturing to her. With a stubborn expression on her face, Marta wrinkles her nose at me, displeased.

"Not from the fight, I hope," Medik says, hurrying over, concern on his face. "If so then you should have commed me a lot sooner."

"No, no, it's not from the fight," I say, and Marta groans, covering her face, which is suddenly very red.

"Arkdhem, go stand over there." She points to the corner. Her cheeks are darkening with color, more than I have seen in all the time we've had together, and I find it both fascinating and incomprehensible. I do not understand why she is changing colors now.

"Why?"

"Because this is embarrassing enough without you

hovering over me." She presses her hands against her face. "Oh my god, just go, please. I can't remember the last time I had anyone join me at a doctor's appointment, especially when I don't actually need an examination."

"If you wish, you may keep the towel covering any part you do not wish me to see," Medik says to her seriously. I frown. He needs to see the bruises to ensure I did not do too much damage in my zeal for punishment.

Despite Marta's insistence that she is fine, I want his medical opinion.

"Thank you, I will." Marta looks at me again and for the first time I see that she truly is uncomfortable and does not wish my presence so close to her. "Please go stand in the corner?"

When she uses that pleading note, I cannot deny her.

Sighing inwardly, I go to the corner where she indicated, glancing over my shoulder as Medik bends over her.

"Marta, do you have any particularly bad aches or sore spots?" Medik asks.

I bite my tongue, because he's asking her, not me, but it's difficult.

"Not really. I really am fine."

"How about you let me look at the worst of it, just to soothe Arkdhem's nerves?"

I scowl into the corner, but I don't protest. Whatever will prompt her to let him examine her.

"Oh, fine," she mutters, and I hear the rustling of fabric.

I glance over my shoulder to see what she's showing him —the towel that's wrapped around her has been lifted to show an ample curve of buttock. The dark coloring of bruises over her skin makes me wince. She isn't as pale as Dawn, but that portion of her skin is lighter than the rest, and the bruises stand out more clearly.

There is a part of me that loves seeing my marks on her.

That part makes me very uncomfortable. I do not want to harm her, after all, even for punishment.

"See? It's not that bad." Marta's voice is indignant at having to suffer through Medik's examination, and my lips quirk. She is a fiery spirit, my Marta.

Medik lifts his head and his eyes meet mine, amusement dancing in them. One of his hands rests on Marta's hip, fingertips on the nanotech belt.

"Arkdhem, she truly is fine. Certainly, you have not—"

Mid-sentence, Medik flickers. Not just him, Marta too.

What the frakk?

I'm already in motion, but it's too late. They flicker again, looks of surprise on their face, and then they both disappear.

"Marta! Medik! Marta!" I run forward, throwing myself at the bed where my Tribute rested only a moment before. The impression of her body is still there, on the sheets, but she is gone, and my hands fall through the space where she'd rested only moments before.

Sheer panic guts me.

What just happened?

How?

Why?

I howl with all the savage terror coursing through me, my armor shooting to pure black, flashing with jagged edges of sickening reds and yellows.

The door opens behind me, but I cannot look, do not hear the shouts of the warriors tumbling into the room to find me throwing the bedding around, as if I might find her somehow hidden beneath it. My chest is too tight around my rapidly beating heart as one thought pounds through my head, over and over again.

She's gone, she's gone, she's gone.

 *arta*

I DON'T REMEMBER what the sensation of going through the wormhole while I was dying, but I imagine it is something like this. I feel like I'm being squeezed, suffocated, and pulled apart all at once. Like my body is being stretched in every direction, so completely that my molecules are about to go careening into different directions as I explode, only to suddenly be compressed again, into too small a space.

When it abruptly ends, I vomit—right down onto the gleaming floor in front of me. How I immediately know it's different from a Tsenturion floor, I have no idea, but I do.

Jabol. That looks like the floor from Frllil's lab.

Horror jabs through me as the obvious conclusion lurches through my mind, despite how splintered and disjointed my thoughts are.

Dumbass, dumbass, dumbass.

"What is the meaning of this?" Medik's voice is loud. So

loud. I wince as I raise my head. He's pushing himself up to his feet, swaying on them, but he manages to move in front of me, like he's trying to protect me.

On the other side of him, I can see Jabol. Four of them. Is one of them Frllil? I have no idea. They all look exactly alike. Even more so than the Tsenturion warriors, who at least have defining features. How do you tell one blob of Jello apart from another?

Easy answer—you don't.

I can't tell if one of them is Frllil.

"Who is that? How did he come with her? Is that her mate?" One of the Jabol quivers. Can a blob quiver with indignation? I moan slightly, trying to push myself up the same way Medik has, not wanting to be on the ground in front of hostile aliens, clutching the towel to my breasts.

"No, that is the Tsenturion Medik." One of the other blobs bobbles forward and somehow, now that he's spoken, I recognize Frllil. The dirty little traitor. I glare at him, but he doesn't seem to notice me. "He was touching her nanotech when she was transported."

My brain feels like it's working in a haze of fog, but I get what he's saying—the nanotech is how they were able to teleport me. That's scary as hell. Does that mean Pareena and Dawn are vulnerable too?

"He is unnecessary," the first Jabol says. "Eliminate him."

A blast of light shoots from one of the other Jabol and hits Medik squire in the chest and I scream as Medik falls in front of me, dropping to my knees, no longer caring about the towel. There is a large hole burned into his armor, which seems like it's trying to rapidly repair itself.

"No," I whisper, my shock and horror freezing me in place, hands hovering over the gaping wound. Something stings my eyes, and it's not until I feel the wetness on my cheeks that I realize I'm crying. "No, Medik... no..."

He smiles, and for a moment I think he's going to be okay, despite everything.

"Sala…" He breathes the word out like it's a benediction, his eyes closing.

I wait, and wait, and wait, but his eyes don't open again, and his chest is still. He's gone. He's truly, actually gone, cut down in front of me without an ounce of compassion or care for him as a person. They fucking Cedric Diggory-ed him.

"No." I whimper the word, tears sliding down my cheeks unchecked.

The sound comes roaring back into my ears and I can hear Frllil yelling. But it's too late. It's far too late.

"You said you wanted her for questioning! No one was supposed to be hurt! This is unthinkable!"

Oh Frllil. You poor, deluded asshole. I close my eyes, choking on the sob that's trying to work its way out of my throat. It doesn't take a genius to figure out what happened.

He went to his Illumination Guides and either asked the wrong questions, or told them enough that they became suspicious. Wanted to talk to me. And he'd been wrong about them. So, so wrong.

I would feel sorry for him if he wasn't so damn stupid. He's gotten Medik killed. Anger sweeps through me. Rage. All accompanied by a helplessness that makes me want to scream.

"He was unnecessary. Stand back, Frllil. You have clearly been diverted from your path by interaction with these lower forms. We will guide you back to the One True Path, as we are meant to do."

Frllil bristles, or as close as he can to such a thing.

"There is no One True Path! What are you talking about?"

"Silence, Frllil." The first Jabol's edges roll in a way that nauseates me and seems vaguely threatening somehow. I press my lips together, leaning against Medik's body, still trying to figure out what to do. If there is anything I can do. "We are the Guides. We have found the One True Path. We will show you the way."

What was vaguely threatening now comes out as outright intimidation.

Frlil quivers, falling back silently.

There will be no help from him. I am all alone.

* * *

Arkdhem

Marta is gone.

I rock back and forth on my bed, the gaping hole in the center of my chest unbearable. It is like losing Tsentur all over again, but far worse... any hope for the future that I'd had left is gone—ripped from me, and I don't know by whom, or how to get her back.

The only thing that keeps me from throwing myself out the airlock is the tiny bit of the bond that still tethers us together. I can feel her. Or I am fooling myself. But I am almost sure I can feel her. And as long as she is alive, I might be able to get her back.

And if I don't, then I will hunt down whoever has taken her to the ends of the universe and take my revenge, no matter what the High Commander has to say about it.

"It must be the Vgotha again!" Corin growls the words, one of his arms around me in support.

"No way," Dawn protests from her spot beside the High Commander. "They wouldn't. Besides, how would they have? When they took me, and when they took me and Pareena, there were battles. Not people disappearing without a trace. That's something the Jabol do."

"My Tribute is right." The High Commander's voice is hard and full of determination. "The Vgotha, for all their tactics and technology, have never been able to transport anyone in such a manner. The Jabol, on the other hand…"

"That is not proof," Corin argues, his arm tight around my shoulders, as though he is determined to hold me together by sheer force of will. He is a good friend, but I am hardly in a mindset to truly appreciate it. "The Vgotha's tech has been growing, we may not have seen everything they are capable of. Every time we turn around, they have something new."

"He's not wrong," Bogdan points out. For once, the second's presence doesn't grate on me. I don't care about him.

I only care about Marta.

The bed beneath me shifts slightly, and I lift my head to see Pareena taking a seat next to me. She is close, though not touching, her dark eyes full of sympathy that hurts to see because it means there is reason for it. Because Marta is gone.

"Can you feel her, Arkdhem? Through the bond?"

"Only enough to know she is alive." My voice is hoarse from screaming, the words rasping out of me from a pained throat. And yet nothing hurts as badly as the emptiness of my arms. "For now."

"Hey now, no defeatist attitude." Dawn approaches me from the front. Unlike Pareena, she has no hesitation in crouching down in front of me and putting her hand on my knee. But then, Gavrill and I have a very different relationship than Bogdan and I. The warmth of her hand does nothing to alleviate the coldness gripping me from the inside out. "If she's alive, we can get her back."

"Can we?" The bitter words fall from my lips. "Can you guarantee that? Because I know—all we Tsenturions know—

there are some things we cannot change. Some things we can never recover."

Silence falls as the mass grief of the warriors fills the room, the thread that has always connected us since the destruction of Tsentur, no matter our differing views on anything else. No matter how Bogdan and I disagree, no matter how we fight, there has always been that common connection between us, between all of us. It is something Dawn and Pareena cannot truly grasp, and I am glad of it for their sake.

There is a long moment and then Dawn gathers herself, shaking her head.

"Look, I can't know what you went through, but I know if I were Marta, I would be pissed as hell that you'd given up on me before all hope was lost. Yeah?"

My mate is fiery. A fighter. A survivor.

All she has already lived through has proven that.

Dawn has a point.

I gather myself, looking up at Gavrill, asking him as a fellow Tsenturion and not as one of his warriors. "Permission to leave my quarters." The gravel in my voice adds to the hollowness of my tone. "We need to find who took my Marta."

"Permission granted. Let's go to the bridge."

MARTA

HUDDLED AGAINST MEDIK'S BODY, I have to push back against my grief. I cling to him, unwilling to move away until I absolutely have to, trying to get my brain working again and looking around the space where I've landed. There has to be something I can do. Something I can use.

I remember accepting my death when I was trapped beneath rubble on earth and bleeding out. This isn't the case now. I can still move. I'm surrounded by crazy ass tech. There has to be something I can do, even if it's taking these fuckers down with me.

My death will *not* be meaningless.

The room is circular, and there's a slight humming vibration beneath my legs, indicating that we're on a ship. There are no windows, but there are a lot of screens in the room around us, all showing different diagrams and things that I can't read.

Frllil is moving steadily away from the rest of the Jabol, shrinking back into a corner. I resist the urge to scream at him to do something. I already trusted him once. I won't make that mistake again.

The other three Jabol are arguing in the center of the room, one of them pushing at a console and clearly becoming increasingly frustrated.

"Why isn't it working?" he trills, turning his focus to Frllil, who shrinks back again.

"The nanotech was always meant to bond the Tribute to the Warrior," he squeaks. "In doing so, it seems to have undergone enough changes at a metaphysical level that it no longer responds to our initial tech. The only reason it was possible with Marta is because she is the newest of the Tributes, and the tech has only changed a little since she was delivered to the Tsenturions."

Is it my imagination, or does he glance at me after he speaks? Either way, I do feel a little better knowing these assholes can't get their hands on Dawn and Pareena. Not for lack of trying.

The three immediately fall to arguing about how they

might be able to recover Dawn and Pareena. It's clear they mean to use the Tributes to force the Tsenturions to do their bidding. What's worse, I'm pretty sure it will work. That must be why they were in such a hurry to match the highest ranking officers to Tributes—it wasn't just an acknowledgement of their rank, it was a backup plan.

I'm seething, scanning my eyes across everything, looking for something I can use... we're definitely on a bridge of some kind, but none of the tech looks like anything the Tsenturions have. It's a lot more like what Frllil had, but all the stuff he wouldn't let me touch—that I actually couldn't touch because it was meant to be used by blobs of Jello, and not bipedals.

Though it feels wrong, I even force myself to look down and subtly scan Medik's body, in hopes that he has something I can use... some kind of weapon, some remnant of his armor.

All the while, the Jabol's argument is getting louder. For a group on the 'One True Path' they don't seem like they have one mindset.

I am sorry, Marta.

The voice sounds like it's inside my head, not in my ear, and I jerk upright.

The Jabol aren't looking at me or Frllil, and he's off to the side. Something is tossed to me, and I automatically reach up to catch it. It looks like a small stick.

"What was that?" one of the Jabol asks, his body quivering. How much did he see? I can't tell, and I squeeze the thing against me, huddling closer to Medik.

I am sorry, Marta. You must tell them to fire immediately. When you get back. Tell them, fire immediately. It is important.

"What was that?" the Jabol demands, one of them moving closer to Frllil, the other towards me.

Fire immediately. It's important.

And then the world goes black again.

* * *

Arkdhem

WE'RE WATCHING the recording of Marta disappearing from my quarters all over again, my jaw clenched against the unruly emotions rushing through me, when something begins to flicker in the center of the bridge. Several warriors shout, their armor coming up. Alarms ring in our ears.

"Stop!" I roar. I recognize the look. The flickers.

In the center of the waving air, two forms appear: Marta on her knees, Medik on his back.

"Fire immediately…" Her voice is a whisper as I reach her, pulling her into my arms, almost unable to believe she's really there.

"What?"

"Fire immediately!"

Her voice coincides with another shout.

"High Commander! A Jabol ship just appeared on our screens! It is armed!"

"Fire immediately!" Gavrill's command repeats Marta's words, and then she shakes herself, her face and expression clearing, as if coming out of a daze.

"Wait!" she cries out. "Frllil is still on there!"

But it's too late.

Fiery explosions appear on the screens and I pull her into my arms, pressing her face into my chest so she can't see the Jabol's ship exploding… and it's only when Dawn screams that I look down and realize everything we have lost.

Medik has not moved, not because he is dazed or injured… there is a single wound gaping open in his chest

166

that his nanotech has not even tried to repair because no repair is possible. There is no point.

Medik is dead.

I hold Marta tighter to me, this new loss pulsing through me and doubling the anguish between us. It does not erase my joy at having her back in my arms, but it exists alongside it… one hole has been closed, and another has opened.

"No! Medik! *No!*" Gavrill falls to his knees beside Medik's body, his voice broken because he already knows the truth.

All around the bridge, warriors are falling to their knees as a grief that we thought was buried tsencycles ago is reawakened, the bridge awash with armor in flickering blues and greys, reflecting our mourning. Dawn wraps her arms around Gavrill from behind, tears streaming down her face. I rock Marta against me as she sobs, my own tears joining hers.

The man who served as father to all the warriors since Tsentur was destroyed, is gone.

CHAPTER 17

 _arta_

I WAS WRONG ABOUT FRLLIL. He wasn't a worthless coward. He saved me, and sacrificed himself. And the guilt of knowing that my thoughts about him before his death were so insulting is eating me as much as the guilt of being so useless in the face of danger. I should have saved myself. I should have saved him, and Medik, and… instead, I was the ultimate damsel in distress, saved by outside forces.

Once I handed the little stick thing over to the High Commander, I curled up onto Arkdhem's lap and did my best to shut out the world—like the useless human being I was. Arkdhem carried me back to his rooms and I fell asleep, unable to face reality for a moment longer.

As I came awake, there was a murmur across the room.

I open my eyes to see Arkdhem standing in front of his vid screen, the High Commander on the other screen, both of them talking softly to each other. Does this mean Arkdhem is still going to be undergoing trial?

Tears well in my eyes. I seriously will fall apart if I have to take one more hit.

You think you haven't already fallen apart?

Ignoring the mean little voice in my head, I push up to a sitting position. Seeing the movement out of the corner of his eye, Arkdhem immediately glances over to me and then says something to the High Commander before turning off the screen. As he approaches the bed, I curl up into a little ball, and his expression turns sympathetic.

I can feel his grief in my center, a pulsing ball of unhappiness that is even greater than my own.

"Medik… Frllil…"

"They're both gone." Arkdhem sits on the edge of the bed, his own loss heavy in his eyes, and I scoot closer to him.

"Frllil was one of the good ones," I say, leaning into him. Arkdhem immediately pulls me onto his lap. My muscles respond the way they always do, relaxing into him, even though I don't deserve the comfort. "It's not fair."

"It is not fair, but this is war," Arkdhem says.

"Will you declare war on the entire Jabol race?"

"Frllil sent a data pack over with you. Only a small portion of the Jabol were responsible, but they were allowed to continue with their 'research' by the leaders. The general populace had no knowledge of what was going on. But examples must be made. Gavrill has sent Tsenturion ships to the Jabolian system."

I clutch his hand. "They're not going to…"

Arkdhem shakes his head.

"We will not destroy their entire system or any of their planets. But we will take out the military outposts we had created for them, and the weapons stores they had acquired for us. We'll also disseminate the data Frllil provided so the Jabol know what was sanctioned without their knowledge and be given the truth of their leaders, and then we will leave. What happens next will be up to them, and whether or not they believe us." He pauses for a moment. "The leaders of those who believed in the 'One True Path' were all killed onboard Frllil's ship. I don't know how he managed to get all that information to you, but he did."

"What about the Vgotha?"

"The Vgotha have a choice. They can seek revenge against their former enslavers. But after all this time, they might just want peace."

"I hope so. I don't think the entire race is evil. Frllil wasn't."

"Frllil was very brave. We are still working on decoding all the information he had on the device you gave us."

"What do you think is on it?" I ask, and then immediately feel guilty again for that little bit of curiosity. People—well, aliens, but still people to me—are dead, and I want to know what data one of them left behind.

A sick feeling surges through my stomach.

"I don't know, but I'm looking forward to finding out." His hands sweep over my hair and I wonder how much of my own feelings he can sense. Not much, I hope. "Frllil will not have died in vain. We will decode and use all of the data he's sent us. Already, he has saved both the Tsenturions and the Jabol. If not for the bravery he showed and the information he sent, I think the High Commander would have shown far less mercy to the Jabol population."

Well, that's something at least. Innocents won't die because of a message that I passed along.

I cling to that bit of knowledge as Arkdhem continues to cuddle me.

"Medik's funeral is in a cycle; do you want to go?" he asks

softly, his voice gentle, as if he's telling me I don't have to if I don't want to.

And I don't want to, but I think I need to.

"Yes," I whisper. But I don't move. I let him hold me in the dim lighting of the room, letting his presence and his comfort keep the rest of the world away for just a little while longer.

* * *

Marta

As I stand beside Arkdhem in a sea of Tsenturion warriors, the air of sadness is palpable. Their communal grief chokes me, amplifying my guilt. I should have done something to try to save Medik. Anything. He wasn't even supposed to be there—only I was.

Gavrill leads the funeral proceedings from a raised platform in the middle of the crowd. Dawn is by his side with a bowl of flowers in her hands. Pareena stands across from Dawn, holding another, identical bowl. Bogdan looms behind her. The room is full of dark grey armor, tinged with blue. It is a beautiful color, but sad, and my eyes tear up at the very sight of it.

"At all our previous funerals, Medik was up there with them," Arkdhem murmurs, his voice tight. "He served as father to all of us, after we lost ours, and now we serve as his sons, in place of those he lost."

My throat and face are tight as a slow procession of warriors carries a pall bearing Medik's body up to the raised platform. I swallow and clear my throat several times, but the knot isn't dissipating.

"To all those gathered, we remember the fallen," Gavrill

intones. "We honor our dead. The many we have lost. Remember them well."

I jump as everyone around me responds, "We will remember."

Arkdhem's hand is on my shoulder. I raise mine and squeeze it tight. Now that funerals are so rare, each one is a reminder of the destruction of their planet. It's a chance to reflect on that huge loss.

How did the warriors grieve the genocide of their race? Did Medik hold a ceremony like this? Or did the warriors simply pick up and move on, numbing themselves with duty, trying to forget?

They couldn't focus on their duties, though. They were warriors who had made it their life's mission to protect the weak. And they could not protect what was most sacred to them.

No wonder the Jabol's manipulation worked. The High Commander must have jumped on the chance to give his warriors a new purpose. And now they've fulfilled one purpose—justice against those who destroyed Tsentur—but lost the other. There will be no more Tributes without the Jabol.

Medik was an integral part of the Tribute Program, as well.

Both died together.

Arkdhem touches my shoulder. "It is time." He hands me a tray with a medical scanner, and a few other tools Medik used.

Dawn and Pareena have each done their part of the ceremony. Pareena sprinkled water over Medik's still form in a symbolic cleansing. And Dawn surrounded Medik's body with flowers.

Now it's my turn. I climb the stairs and lay the tray of Medik's tools at his feet.

"We remember the fallen's chosen duty," Gavrill says to the crowd. "How he served us all."

"We remember," the crowd responds.

I bite my lip. Dammit. I blink a bunch of times, moving blindly back to where Arkdhem waits. He folds his arms around me and I snuggle against him, wanting to hide.

He ducks his head close. "You did well."

I shake my head a little.

"What is it?" he asks.

"I can't stop thinking like a reporter. It's easier when I can be a watcher. Removed from all this." I wave a hand, feeling lame. "Just a reporter." I'd still had occasional survivor's guilt, but it hadn't been like this.

Arkdhem takes my hand in both of his. "You are not only a reporter, my Marta," he says simply. "You never were. And now you are my mate. We are bonded and our grief, as well as our joys, are shared."

Dammit, I don't want to cry. I grit my teeth and nod, and focus on the proceedings. Arkdhem keeps watching me closely, though.

Gavrill and the women have left the platform. It rises up over us all, folding over Medik's body. Turning into a small space craft.

The small funeral craft rises and hovers in the air before gently moving towards the end of the hull. The air shimmers briefly as an airlock activates, sealing us off from the funeral craft.

The Tsenturions turn as one. The small ship bearing Medik's body is still drifting towards the back of the hull. Then the doors open and the ship exits the hull. My ears pop, and I cling to Arkdhem to steady myself. The seal keeps us all from being sucked out of space, but we can still watch the funeral craft drift into the emptiness beyond.

"It's like a Viking funeral," I murmur.

"What is that, my Marta?" Arkdhem leans down.

"A Viking funeral. Um... The Vikings were another warrior culture back on Earth," I explain. "At least, we think that's what they were... They didn't really write anything down." I'm babbling. "Anyway, I should shut up and just watch."

In the space beyond, the rest of the Tsenturion fleet has lined up to make a corridor of ships. Medik's funeral craft floats between them, heading to the stars beyond. Like a Viking funeral, but in space.

As the funeral craft reaches the end of the corridor, streams of light shoot out of the nearest Tsenturion space-ships and lock onto the small craft. A bright flare from the explosion, and the tiny ship bearing Medik's body is gone, destroyed by the weapons. There's nothing left but space dust. I gasp, a tremor running through me.

"He's with his mate and family now," Arkdhem murmurs.

"Meu deus." I turn away, a hand over my mouth. Arkdhem cradles me against his body. I'm glad we're not up in the front but in the back because a shocking wave of *something* washes over me. My face feels tight. I gulp for air, but my lungs feel too small. I'm about to be sick. What is happening? Is this grief?

Arkdhem softly strokes my back.

"I don't cry about things," I say through stiff lips. "This isn't me. But..." Ugh, my words are stuck in my throat. I'm about to vomit... or something. I clutch my chest and bend double.

And then the words burst out. *"It's my fault!"*

I claw at Arkdhem. *Get me out.*

He scoops me up and carries me to the back of the hall. My face flames, but the warriors simply part to make way, and no one stares at me.

Arkdhem sets me down in a quiet corner where everyone's backs are to us. I'm shaking. Something weird has happened to my body—my insides are like knives, cutting me.

Arkdhem cups my face and leans down so he's all I see. "Tell me."

"It's my fault," I choke out. "It's my fault he's dead."

"No, my Marta. It was the Jabol's fault. Not Frllil's," he amends because he knows that I don't like lumping Frllil in with his evil supervisors, "but Frllil's superiors. They and they alone are to blame for the deaths."

"But if I hadn't..." I trace my actions back through everything. If I hadn't sent Arkdhem away... If I hadn't been embarrassed at my appointment with Medik...

"Perhaps it is my fault, then," Arkdhem says as if reading the line of my thoughts. "I brought Medik to you. When Frllil's superiors tried to retrieve you, anyone touching you would have gone. It is my fault that I was not holding you at that moment. If I had also been taken, I could have slashed through any enemies." He looks like he wants to fight someone, right now.

I tremble a little, my face feels stiff. "You don't know if that would have happened. They could have killed you. Medik was hardly weak. The Jabol had a weapon prepared that decimated his armor." Now I really am going to be sick. If I had lost Arkdhem...

"And they could have killed you," he counters.

"But if I hadn't been asking questions and gotten Frllil to dig for more information in the Archives..."

"Then things might have happened another way—a worse way. The Jabol committed atrocities. We were always going to come to war, and all involved would be at risk." He pauses. "Unless you wish that the Tsenturions never found out the truth—"

"No, no." My stomach has calmed down. Under Arkd-hem's comforting touch, I relax a little.

He lets me stand frozen for a minute, then asks gently, "Have you thought through all the possibilities sufficiently? Can you lay to rest this blame? Does blaming yourself honor Medik or Frllil's death?"

"No," I admit.

He touches my cheek, right under my eye. His finger comes away wet.

"I don't cry," I parrot. "I don't cry at things like this."

Arkdhem wraps his powerful arms around me. I let him cuddle me to his chest. "Perhaps this time, you do."

* * *

MARTA

A NEW PLATFORM has risen up to replace the one that left, and Pareena climbs the stairs to address the crowd.

"And now I'd like to welcome anyone who wishes to come up, one by one, and share a story about Medik. If you want to. You can say what he meant to you. Let's lift up his memory and remember him as he'd want us to. Then we can grieve and live our lives—which he'd want us to do."

As soon as she steps away, Bogdan climbs up the stairs. He looks as surly and fierce as ever, but when his gaze touches on his mate, it softens.

"I will start," he says in a begrudging way that makes me think that Pareena put him up to this. "Medik... when I received my Tribute, I did not know how to bond with her. I did not know what to do with her. Through my grief for my lost family and through my rebirth as my Tribute's mate, he counseled me. He stood in my father's shoes and guided me, the way a father would." Another pause with even more glowering, as if he resented having to share his emotions. "That is my memory of Medik."

Yeah, Pareena definitely put him up to this. But it works. There now a line of Tsenturions forming at the stairs.

"Thank you for sharing," Pareena murmurs, and motions for the next warrior to ascend the platform.

I hug Arkdhem's waist. The giant wave of grief has passed, and I don't feel like crying anymore. Down in the crowd, I can see Dawn leaning against her mate. She's broken down into full-on waterworks, but she gets a pass because she's pregnant. Not like me, who broke down even though I don't really have a right to.

Pareena's cheeks are wet but she's in her element, helping others process their emotions, helping them through their grief. Unlike me, she's useful, and the warriors respond to her, letting her comfort them.

A memory pings at me as I listen to the stories the warriors tell of Medik. The last thing Medik said to me. I'd almost forgotten, with everything that happened immediately afterwards.

"Arkdhem... What is Sala?"

"Sala? Sala was Medik's mate's name."

And just like that, I choke on tears again.

CHAPTER 18

*M*_{*arta*} The memorial service has just ended when Arkdhem bends down to whisper in my ear, "Marta, will you come with me? There's something you should see."

"Now?" All I want to do is go back to our rooms and lie in bed. Not move. Not think. Maybe sleep some more. Unconsciousness is bliss.

"Yes."

But he wouldn't ask if it weren't really important. I duck my head and let him pull me down the hallway.

"The communication officers contacted me just before the service. They've broken through the encoding in Frllil's device," Arkdhem tells me.

"What? Why didn't you say?" I quicken my steps, pushing aside my melancholy. My curiosity has always been my driving force, and I feel an overwhelming need to know what was on that device. Arkdhem picks up the pace, and by the time we reach the communications deck, we're jogging. Of course, I'm out of breath, and he's not.

We enter a small, darkened antechamber, and cross

immediately to a door. Arkdhem lays his hand on the side of the wall to request entry.

The lights dim even further, and Arkdhem squeezes my hand.

"Why is it dark?" I ask in a hushed tone.

"It's part of the decryption. Apparently, the information is light sensitive."

A second later, a whooshing sound signals that the door in front of us has glided open. The room beyond is much larger, and lit with a 3D model that's glowing, suspended in the middle of the room. Arkdhem ushers me in and the door closes behind us, keeping in the darkness. There are two Tsenturions to the left of us, but my eyes are fixed on the model of a galaxy in front of us. The spiral pattern hangs in the air, rotating slowly. The center is bright yellow, but the tendrils are pale white. Almost a milky color…

Is that what I think it is?

"What have you found?" Arkdhem asks. His hands come to my shoulders, steadying me. I put a hand over his large one.

"It took a day-cyle to realize dark-light would help us decrypt the code," one of the communications officer says almost apologetically. "But from there, it was easy. The data contains one thing: a map to a particular star system."

"Oh my god…" I breathe out the words, and immediately bite my lip. It's too soon to tell, isn't it? The Milky Way can't be entirely unique in its appearance, in the whole universe.

As the Tsenturion speaks, the image before us rotates and then starts to get larger, as if someone clicked a button to make us zoom in.

"Which star system?" Arkdhem asks as the galaxy spirals grow bigger and then disappear on the periphery of the image.

"It's not one that our systems recognize. It's incredibly far away. The map centers on a particular star—you can see it here." A point in the image grows bigger, becoming a familiar-looking glowing orb circled by a few multicolored dots. "It has nine planets... well, eight planets? It's kind of hard to tell with that last one."

I gasp. "*Meu deus!*"

It is! That's it!

"Marta? What is it?" Arkdhem steadies me as I point.

"That's our system! That's Earth!" The image of my home planet is suspended in front of us. It looks familiar: two icy points at either end, and blue and brown continents in between. There's Ecuador, in the middle.

I stare at my home planet, and there's an ache deep inside me.

"How far away?" Arkdhem asks, seeming to realize that I've been struck speechless.

The IT Tsenturion clears his throat. "Far. It would take us at least two tsencycles to reach it. But the data contains clear instructions on how to navigate the wormhole. Once we reach the galaxy, we can find Earth."

I put a hand to my lips, a gesture my mother did often when she was surprised. "I can't believe it. We can go back! Dawn, Pareena, and I—we—can all go home!"

Arkdhem squeezes my shoulders as he asks the IT guy, "Rodion, do the instructions include temporal coordinates as well?"

Rodion babbles something I don't understand about wormholes and coordinates.

"What does that mean?" I turn to Arkdhem.

I can't see his face in the darkness, but he sounds very grave as he says, "It means you can return home, and only a few years will have passed on Earth. Without temporal coordinates, we would return to your planet centuries later."

My mouth falls open. "Right. Wormholes."

I'm no physicist, but faster than light travel would have some effect on time, wouldn't it?

Arkdhem's large hand passes over my hair. "A way back to your planet. Frllil left you this for a reason."

"His final gift." My eyes sting. I'm glad it's dark in here.

"We're done decrypting the data, if you wish to turn on the lights," Rodion says.

"Um, yeah." I dash my fingers over my face. I seem to be suffering from an excess of emotion. Again. My body is hot and cold all over.

Must. Not. Cry.

Maybe I'm just overwhelmed. I never thought I would be able to go back home. When the lights come back up, I whirl to Arkdhem and grab him. "Isn't this amazing?" I gush. "We can go back home!"

We can tell our friends and family that we didn't die. Introduce the Tsenturions to human women, the human way instead of through abduction. Use their technology to save our planet. Use our women to save their race. So much good could come from this. For the first time since Medik was killed in front of me, I feel joy. Hope.

God, we really could change worlds. Universes.

"Yes," he replies softly. His face is strangely blank, his eyes hollow.

"I can't believe it," I repeat. I want to run around the ship, shouting for joy. "This is going to be so great."

And yet, there's still a hollow ache at the center of my chest, but I push it aside. It's only natural that some grief should linger, despite this momentous news.

For some reason, it doesn't occur to me that it might be Arkdhem's ache I'm feeling.

More and more, all the implications are coming together in my head, little connections on how beneficial this will be to both races. But we'll have to present it in the right way.

And that will be my job. I'm going to be the one to break the story, and introduce the Tsenturions to the humans.

* * *

Arkdhem

MY TRIBUTE IS SO happy as we return to my quarters. The bond between us bubbles over with her excitement. Her cheeks are a shining pink. She's muttering to herself now.

"I could break the news through the BBC, or maybe the New York Times. They snubbed me for my last article, though. So maybe I'll choose the LA Times instead. Or the Washington Post. Just to stick it to them, the snooty bastards. This will have to be done carefully, though…" She whirls to me and takes in my subdued expression. "Oh Arkdhem… Is it wrong of me to be so excited? This is the scoop of a lifetime!"

She's practically crowing, and I understand. It is the same way I felt when I was made second-in-command. I can tell how much it means to her.

"Not at all," I answer. Her happiness should be my own, but the taste is bittersweet.

I want her to return to Earth and further her career. I do. But I do not want to be left behind. What will Dawn and Pareena think? Will they be caught up in her excitement, and determined to leave their lives as Tributes as well?

If so, the High Commander and Bogdan are not going to be happy with me.

Although, Dawn and Pareena have been Tributes far longer than Marta has. Their bonds with their mates are deeper. Perhaps they will not have the same impulse to leave so quickly as Marta does.

I rub at my chest, where the ache inside is increasing.

I was so afraid that the High Commander would take her away from me, but it turns out it was not him and my upcoming trial that I had to fear... it is Marta's home planet. And how can I compete with that? If given the opportunity, of course I would want to see Tsentur again.

But you would want her to go with you, wouldn't you?

Yes, of course, but it is different for her. She did not choose to be part of the Tribute Program, not truly. And even if she had, she had no way of truly understanding what she was signing up for.

Flopping down on her back on the bed, she stares up at the ceiling. Despite how energized she was a moment ago, that does not stop the melancholy from creeping back in. I know that only too well.

Duty only takes one so far.

Eventually, you have to stop and feel again.

"I can't believe I thought Frllil was a coward," she whispers, her voice choking up a little.

Getting onto the bed with her, I pull her into my arms, offering her my comfort. I will hold her for as long as I can, until I have to let her go.

* * *

Marta

"All right, Arkdhem. Tell us why we are gathered here," the High Commander says. We're all sitting around a circular table—we three human women and our mates, plus the Tsenturion Rodion, who was one of the IT specialists who cracked Frllil's encryption.

It's only been a few hours since the memorial service ended. Dawn and Pareena are still red-eyed from crying, and my own eyes still feel scratchy. Arkdhem insisted on the meeting, telling everyone it was important.

Bogdan has his arms folded over his chest. He's glowering at Arkdhem.

My mate is unfazed. "My Marta has something to announce." He touches my arm.

"Well, Rodion and I," I pipe up. "He's the one who figured out the encryption."

"What encryption?" Dawn looks puzzled.

"There was more information encoded on the disc Frllil gave to Marta," the High Commander interjects. "More than the information about the Jabol and that One True Path nonsense. Although, I did not know it had been decoded." He raises his eyebrows at Rodion, who shrugs.

"We wanted to be able to give you a full report, and we had to test some of the information. Arkdhem and Marta were essential to us figuring out there was anything worthwhile on it."

"It was his last gift to us." Suddenly, there's a knot in my throat. I swallow around it a few times. Stupid emotion, making me choke up.

There's a sheen to Dawn and Pareena's eyes. It makes me feel a little better.

"Are you saying this message came from the enemy?" Bogdan growls.

"Frllil wasn't the enemy," I blurt, ready to argue. I'm not the only one ready to defend Frllil's memory.

"Don't call him that!" Dawn slams the table. "He was our friend!" Her face screws up, and she looks like she's about to weep. The High Commander puts an arm around her.

"We understand. He is not the enemy," he says soothingly.

Bogdan opens his mouth, probably to argue. We all glare at him.

"Bogdan," Pareena murmurs, and lays a hand on her mate's arm and he concedes defeat.

"Very well. The Jabol Frllil who is not our enemy," he grumbles.

"If your concern is safety, I had the contents thoroughly scanned to be sure there was no weapon," Arkdhem says. "The message was simply information. Rodion can explain the security protocols."

"Yes, allow me to explain." Rodion launches into a bunch of technical jargon as if he's been waiting for his moment. The High Commander looks vaguely interested but he keeps glancing down at his mate. Dawn looks tired, poor thing, and I'm sure Rodion's droning voice isn't helping.

Pareena nods like she's listening but her eyes are starting to glaze over. So are mine.

"Perhaps we can save the full explanation for later," Arkdhem cuts into Rodion's rambling. "Let Marta tell you the important details."

I squeeze my mate's hand gratefully. The smile he showers on me is almost... sad. It makes me pause.

Lately, my mate has been quiet. At his end of our bond, there's a flicker of something like... loneliness? Even despair. I'm going to have to figure out what's going on there. But first, I'm excited to share this news.

"Marta?" Arkdhem prompts.

"Um, yes. The point is, Frllil left us a message. Rodion and his team worked on decrypting it."

"We weren't sure what we had found, though, until Arkdhem brought Marta to us," Rodion continues, giving me a wide smile. Our lack of interest in the technical details doesn't seem to have fazed him at all. "To us, it was just a random map and coordinates."

"What map and coordinates?" Pareena asks, sitting up straight.

Rodion activates a display in the center of us, but it's not the same as before. He's been hard at work the past few hours, and he's apparently recalibrated it so he can show us the map in the light. The galaxy, as I saw it before, appears, and then there's a zooming feature that makes me feel a little motion sick before Earth blinks into view.

Dawn gasps, covering her belly with her hand. "Is that what I think it is?"

Pareena looks blank. Next to her, Bogdan is frowning, but as far as I can tell, he has resting dick face.

"It's Earth," I confirm. "And there are coordinates. That's what the map is. It gives us a way back. We can go home." I throw my hands up in the air, beaming. If I had confetti, I'd be tossing it.

Silence.

I glance around at the faces, but no one seems excited. What the fuck?

Then Dawn bursts into tears. Loudly, noisily.

"Give us a moment," Gavrill says, and scoops her up and exits the room.

Pareena doesn't seem surprised by the outburst. At all. "Let's take a break," she announces, and turns to her mate.

I'm already rising out of my chair. Arkdhem follows me to the corner of the room, where I punch the replicator buttons to order a cup of *cafezinho*—or a beverage as close to sweet black coffee as the replicator can make.

"That is not the response I was expecting," I grumble. "I thought they'd all be happy about it."

"Give them time," Arkdhem replies softly. He sounds so sad, I whirl around.

"Arkdhem, what is wrong? What aren't you telling me?"

"Nothing is wrong," he says stiffly. "I am happy that you can return to Earth."

A whisper of loneliness echoes in our bond. *Don't leave me.*

And it all becomes clear. He thinks I want to return to Earth alone.

"Oh, no." I take his hand. "You misunderstand. I don't want to leave you."

"No?"

"Of course not. Why would you think that? You're my mate." I take a deep breath. Emotions aren't my favorite thing, but I need to convince him. Show him that he matters to me. I could have died without him ever knowing how I felt about him, and I wasn't okay with that. "You're the other half of my heart. Anything we do, we do together."

arta

By the time Gavrill and Dawn return, I've made a bunch of cookies and tea for everyone and set it out. Rodion sits down and awkwardly takes a cup, holding it in his hands rather than trying to drink from it, like he's not quite sure what he's supposed to do with it.

Mentally, I put human mannerism and etiquette classes for the warriors on my to-do list.

"Sorry about that," Dawn says, cradling a cup of tea. She smiles a little weakly. "I'm just emotional."

"Understandable," Pareena says. "It's a lot to take in." She's sitting directly on Bogdan's lap, calmly dunking a cookie into her tea. "Especially after coming to terms with the thought of living with the Tsenturions for the rest of your life. The chance to go home is almost overwhelming."

"Sorry, guys," I say. "I should've broken it to you more gently. I thought it was good news."

"It is good news," Pareena says. "There are things I miss about Earth. It would be good to see my family and friends again. To let them know I didn't die."

"But what about our mates?" Dawn blurts. Gavrill covers her hand with his own.

"If you wish to go home, I will not stop you," he says.

She shakes her head, more tears in her eyes. "There's no way I'm leaving you. I made our choice long ago."

"*Meu deus*," I burst out. "What do you mean, go back without our Tsenturion mates? Why does everyone keep thinking that's what I meant? We can use the Tsenturion ships to get there. We can all go back—all of us. We can teach the Tsenturions how to date. They can help us save our planet, and the people on it. Better the lives of everyone."

And I can be the reporter who breaks the news, convinces everyone that the aliens aren't there to invade us, and that we should all get along. I have a feeling there will be quite a few alien romance readers who are completely on board with getting to date a six-and-a-half-foot tall gold aliens with tentacle pubes and giant alien penises. Tsenturions are going to go from no hope for their species to too many applicants.

"What about the temporal capabilities?" the High Commander asks, looking at Rodion.

"The temporal capabilities are fine," Rodion jumps in, nodding his head so vigorously that his teacup shakes, spilling some liquid over the sides. Quickly, he puts it down on the table in front of him. "It will take a few human years, but we can get there."

"We need to be careful," Parcena warns thoughtfully. "Humans aren't known for being tolerant of something new. Aliens—real aliens… well, not everyone will be welcoming. Some people can't even handle differences between them and other people, much less an entirely different species."

"Most people will be on board once we show them how

the Tsenturion tech can eradicate disease and increase their technology," I argue. "Trust me, I know exactly how to spin this. That was—is—my job."

"It won't be easy." The High Commander looks thoughtful, turning his attention to me. "We will need a good liaison between the Tsenturions and the human media."

Pareena chuckles. "I would say that Marta is more than up to the job. Not to mention, she wants it. And she's right about being able to present the story in the right way. That's going to be incredibly important."

"And I can interview you as a source," I tell her. "Your credentials are pretty great. You can help explain all this to people in terms they can understand." I give up on playing cool and rub my hands together. "Am I wrong to be excited?"

"No, no," Dawn says, even as her tears are shining on her cheeks. "This is the scoop of a lifetime."

The table erupts in separate conversations. The High Commander questions Rodion, while Arkdhem and Bogdan listen and interject from time to time, while simultaneously listening in on Pareena and Dawn reminiscing about what they'd like to see when they get back. Pareena wants to see her family. Dawn wants to see her grandmother's house. Me? I want to see my editor. Yeah, I've got some issues.

Pareena gets up to make more cookies, and I follow her.

"What are your thoughts on continuing the Bride program?" I ask. "With a few modifications. Make it more like a dating app." I hold up my hands to do fake quotes. "'Swipe right for abduction.'"

"There would have to be several modifications," Pareena says.

"You could put it together," I suggest. "You've been doing enough studies on the Tsenturion males… they're going to need help adapting to human customs. Um, and we may need to get them some new manuals."

Pareena laughs, but her eyes have lit up from within at the thought of this new challenge. I know exactly how she feels.

"Yes... hm... there are quite a few ways I've thought of that would be a good way of helping warriors and Tributes understand each other. I wasn't sure how willing the warriors would be while they had Tributes coming to them one at a time, but on Earth, they'll be on our home turf... hm..." Pareena wanders back towards the table, already deep in thought, and I laugh, returning to Arkdhem's lap and listening to my friends talk about what they remember from Earth.

I don't have any family or friends for Arkdhem to meet, but there are some things I want to show him... and I definitely want to be there for his first experience of moqueca and other Brazilian dishes. There are some things the replicator has *not* been able to duplicate.

* * *

Marta

"Well, that turned out great." I'm still bubbly when we reach our quarters.

"I am glad." Arkdhem still sounds tired.

"Hey." I poke him. "You thought I was going to leave you? I would never leave you."

He sits on the bed and I climb onto his lap, straddling him. His large hands cup my backside. My skin hums with the contact—the nanotech waking up.

"I know that now," he says. His hands move up and down, stroking my butt and my back. I rock slightly, ready to be turned on, but not quite yet. I want to enjoy our closeness.

"What did Gavrill want to talk to you about?" The High

Commander had pulled Arkdhem aside while Pareena and I were discussing alien dating apps.

"The Council met to make a decision, deciding that the trial was unnecessary. It seems I will be relieved of command permanently."

I stiffen. "What?"

Arkdhem continues as if he hasn't just dropped a bomb into the conversation. "I will have plenty of time to support your career." He smiles, though I can see he is conflicted about what he's saying. "I will be the Tsenturion half of the liaison between your people and mine. It is an important job."

"But you won't be a warrior anymore."

"No."

I reach through the bond, trying to gauge how he feels. Sadness. Resignation. But also a kind of determination.

"I'm sorry."

"I'm not," he says softly, stroking my hair back. "I would not change anything that has happened to me, because it brought me to you. This is how Tsenturion life was always supposed to be... the time to be a warrior ends, and the time to have a family begins."

Awww.

"Well, I guess we'll have more time to be together then." I rock forward and rub a little against his cock. A bolt of heat shoots through me, reverberating between us as passion floods the bond. "And make plans for when we get to Earth. Humans aren't exactly known for their calmness in the face of something new. We will have to craft an excellent media campaign to present to world leaders and the news outlets."

"You are the perfect human for the job," he says. "I have the utmost faith in you, my heart."

I hum, rocking a bit faster. Arkdhem's armor has melted away, and his *seela* have somehow ripped apart my garments so they can suction onto my sex. One of them fastens on my clit and pulls in a strong, sucking motion. I moan, melting towards him. Stars burst behind my eyes as my clit is stimulated relentlessly, leaving me shuddering atop him.

"Oh, Arkdhem, that is good," I gasp.

"Call me Master," he orders, and when I do, he lifts me a little and reseats me onto his cock, stroking into me with a body-shuddering thrust. The Bride Trainer is at work, sliding up my stomach to pinch my nipples, and swelling to fill my ass. Ecstasy floods the bond between us. Mine. His.

The connection is so intense, I'm crying. And laughing. I am caught between joy and despair, craving the intimacy between us. Needing it to push back the darkness inside of me.

The *seela* suction onto my legs and pop off as Arkdhem lifts me off his cock, helping him reposition me on his lap.

"No, don't stop. I'm okay." I gulp.

"Do not lie to me." He catches my chin. "Marta. Tell me what you need. Anything, and I will do it."

I swallow.

"I still feel guilty about Frllil. And Medik. I feel guilty that I'm excited about returning to Earth when they're gone... that I get to do things I always wanted to do while they don't." It's survivor's guilt and I know it, but putting a name to it doesn't make the emotions any easier.

"If it had been you, would you want them to stop their lives and doing what they wanted?"

I wrinkle my nose at him. "No, of course not. And I know they wouldn't expect it of me... I just keep feeling like there was something more I should have done."

Arkdhem's eyebrows rise. "More? More than surviving what should have killed you? Not just now, but multiple times?"

"I didn't survive on my own, though, only because Frllil

saved me. Both times. I was useless," I say quietly. I never thought of myself as the damsel in distress, but that's what I'd been. I'd been at the mercy of the universe, and it had chosen to save me, for some reason, but things could have been so different. I'd had no agency, no say, and if it wasn't for Frllil, I wouldn't be here right now.

"You were not useless." Arkdhem sighs in exasperation, shaking his head. "At all times in battle, I must rely on my warrior companions to watch my back. I have been saved by those around me more times than I can count, and I have saved them as well. Does that mean that we are all useless?"

"No, of course not, but that's different. You're relying on each other. No one was relying on me."

"No?" He cocks his head at me, hands sliding up and down my sides. It's not quite an erotic touch, but it's not exactly soothing either. "Frllil was relying on you to pass on his message, both the verbal one and the disk. Without you, his plan would have failed. The Jabol responsible for Tsentur's destruction would have escaped. We might have wreaked our revenge on perfectly innocent Jabol."

"All I did was blurt out a message that got him killed because I was too freaked out to think through what I was saying," I grumble. And then I squeak because suddenly I'm being flipped over. No longer straddling Arkdhem's lap, I find myself over it, butt up in the air, and his big, alien hand caressing my buttocks instead of my side.

Uh oh.

* * *

Arkdhem

. . .

Now that I understand what is plaguing my Tribute, I know what I must do. There is a part of me that hesitates as well, because I had worried about punishing her too harshly before, and that worry led to further events... but I know Medik would happily have given his life to save hers. He would not regret that he ended up on the Jabol ship, and that his death was what spurred Frllil to truly see his superiors for what they were. In some ways, it might have even been a relief to finally be able to lay down his duty and join his family. He had served far beyond what he was supposed to and I would not tarnish either those long years or his final sacrifice by seeing them for anything less than what they were.

He would not want Marta wracked with guilt, or me.

He would want us to have the long years of happiness that Tsenturions used to have.

And I am now the first Tsenturion to retire to civilian life in tsencycles. I will not waste that, and we will live every day in Medik and Frllil's honor, with gratitude for the sacrifices they made for our futures.

"You conveyed the message Frllil asked you to. You did exactly what you were supposed to do."

There's a moment of silence, and I know she doesn't agree with me.

Smack!

My hand tingles where I swatted her.

"Ouch! I didn't say anything!"

"That's right, you didn't. Did you or did you not do what Frllil asked of you?"

"I did." She sighs. Wriggles. "I should have done more, though."

"Says who? Other than you? You were in hostile territory, naked, and weaponless, not to mention disoriented. Medik was unable to defend himself. He may have no longer been a warrior, but he had been, once. He was armored. What do you think you could have done that he couldn't?"

This time, as she thinks over what I've said, I spank her again—much more lightly than before, but still hard enough to sting, and make her wiggle.

"Okay, okay! You have a point!" The words come grudgingly.

"Good girl." Despite everything, I can feel the way she softens against me at the accolade. She is a good girl. "But I am still going to turn your bottom red, and you can think back to this moment every time you start blaming yourself for situations outside of your control. The only person who thinks you should have been able to do more is you, and it is unacceptable that you don't see how much you did do under the circumstances."

CHAPTER 20

M *arta*

WHAT DID I DO?

And would I have expected Dawn or Pareena to have done the same in my position?

Medik hadn't been able to defend himself. Do I really think I could have saved him when he, a full Tsenturion warrior in battle armor, hadn't been able to?

Talk about hubris.

And Frllil... I could never have done what he did. I didn't know how to use Jabol tech in the same way he did. I'm not even sure I had the right parts to do so. I could have never taken down their shields and exposed them to the Tsenturions' scanners. Even if I had, the Tsenturions would have never fired on the Jabol without a reason to do so.

I had given them that reason. They had listened to me because I was a Tribute.

Every time Arkdhem's hand comes down on my bottom, the message is reinforced.

I did everything I could, and I did what I was needed to do.
Smack!

Wriggling, I squirm on Arkdhem's lap, whimpering as he continues to land hard swats on my cheeks. I can feel the heat growing in my bottom, which clenches around the nanotech plug filling me, increasing my erotic discomfort.

And my pussy is so very, very wet—a fact Arkdhem discovers when he reaches around to check. His fingers stroke my sensitive folds, and he chuckles over my head. Pleasure flows through me, turning even my burning bottom into a delicious inferno. I hold my breath, hoping he'll continue to fondle me.

No such luck. He returns to spanking me, but the pain/pleasure switches in my brain have gotten mixed up again. Every stern swat sends heat blooming through my core. My clit pulses. Instead of squirming away, I'm lifting my bottom to meet his swats.

"Have you learned your lesson?"

"Yes, Master," I murmur. My voice comes from far away. I'm floating a little. But then the plug in my bottom starts to grow… and vibrate.

"I think you are enjoying this too much." The plug starts to push in and out of my ass—Arkdhem must be using it to fuck me. "Perhaps I should find a new way to punish you."

At this moment, with my bottom and core a mass of sensation ready to boil over, more punishment sounds *great.*

"Yes, please, Master," I moan. Then I'm lifted and laid back on the bed, my hair spilling around my face. I hiss and try to plant my heels in the mattress, pushing my hips up to keep my poor tortured bottom from touching the blanket.

"Spread your legs." Arkdhem swats the inside of my thighs lightly, and rearranges me with my knees bent and thighs stretched wide. He looms over me, naked and gorgeous. My pussy pulses, needing to be filled—jealous of the thick, hard length in my ass.

Arkdhem's cock protrudes between his legs, his *seela* stretching as if desperate to latch on to me. This delay is as uncomfortable for him as it is for me.

"Keep your legs apart," he orders. "Bound by my will."

I stretch my arms over my head, offering myself up to him. Complete surrender. He pauses, taking in my naked display. My chest is taut, my legs quivering from the strain of spreading my knees wide. My pussy is open to him.

His eyes hood, and then he murmurs my reward. "You are perfect for me."

His large hands come to rest on my inner thighs, spreading them a little further. Then... "Hold still." And he slaps my pussy.

My body jolts, my thighs jerk, but I keep them spread apart. A small smile touches Arkdhem's lips.

Sadist!

"Good girl," he croons. And he smacks my pussy again. This time, the slap barely registers. Heat detonates between my legs and rushes up my front. My lip quivers.

"Master!" I'm teetering on the edge...

And he knows it. "Come." He pats my pussy over and over, light strikes that grow in intensity until the final, hard *Pop!* Pleasure bursts from my clit.

I convulse, sparks flying through my body, sizzling up from the backs of my legs and burning through my torso. My mouth falls open as I cry out.

Arkdhem's weight comes onto me. He pins my wrists and settles his hips on mine, grounding me even as he strokes inside my body. I convulse again. His cock fills me, pushing against the plug that's heated and *vibrating* in my back channel. I'm completely stuffed. My mouth hangs open as if I can gulp extra air, make extra space in my body. But there's no room in my body but for him.

A storm of my cries fill my own ears as Arkdhem pounds me into the bed.

The *seela* suction onto my punished pussy lips. One finds my clit and sucks so hard, I soar to another planet. Planet Pleasure.

When I return to consciousness, Arkdhem is still inside me, but he's stilled. His heavy body rests on mine in delicious weight. His lips brush my face. "Marta. My beautiful one. My mate."

Slowly, I raise my chin and meet his kiss, sipping on his lips. The Bride Trainer has shrunk in my bottom, lessening the feeling of fullness. Still inside me, Arkdhem rolls so I'm draped on top of him, a boneless blanket. Flutters fill my body as I readjust to his still hard cock spearing my pussy. Soon, he'll be up for Round Two, but in the meantime, he's giving me a reprieve. And he's adorable, gazing up at me like I'm the sun he orbits. My cinnamon roll. My secret sadist.

"Thank you for spanking it better," I whisper.

"Anytime." His palm squeezes my heated rear, massaging roughly. I whimper and wriggle closer. It hurts so good. "Kiss me, my heart."

I slant my head and obey, only to break away and breathe against his lips, "I love you."

"And I you," he murmurs. "No matter what the future brings, I will gladly face it. As long as I'm with you."

EPILOGUE

$\mathcal{M}$<u>arta</u>

SEVERAL LIGHTYEARS AND A SPACE/TIME continuum later...

I DID GET the scoop of a lifetime. The news in every country and every language was that aliens are real, and we can meet with them. They are here to help.

Dawn and Pareena both gave birth to the first Tsenturion/human babies on the trip here. Stella and Aadhya—two little girl warriors who already know how to fully form their Tsenturion armor. Gavrill and Bodgan are torn between pride and worry, both hovering, and egging their little warriors on.

I've been busy writing articles and introducing the Tsenturions to all the world leaders. The alien technology and the medical knowledge that Medik left behind has cured most all human diseases, and went a long way to building goodwill between our species.

Arkdhem was relieved of his Tsenturion officer duty permanently, but serves as my bodyguard. We're both human/alien media liaisons. Ambassadors of peace.

And we're expecting our first little one in six months.

The entire Tsenturion race fleet has been able to enter into a human/Tsenturion dating program. There are many men and women who have always dreamed of being mated to an alien, and this is their chance.

The Vgotha also decided to travel to Earth with us, and several of their warriors have entered the dating program. Some of them are fearsome, with wings and tails—but apparently, there are plenty of humans who include 'sexy wings' and 'naughty tail' on their list of dating preferences.

Tor was the first of his people to visit Earth. He fell in love with a second grade school teacher in Jamaica, and they've settled together quite nicely after a few false starts. They live on his ship for half the year, and spend the other half in a Vgotha-sized house near her mother. Tor's favorite food is now curried goat pasties.

Also, the Jabol have elected new leadership. Better leadership. Best of all, they sent a small gift to us. Apparently, before the explosion, Frllil was able to upload his consciousness to a storage facility on a far off moon. The Jabol found it, and sent it to us. Rodion figured out how to download Frllil's consciousness into a robot designed to Frllil's own specifications. He looks exactly like Chris Hemsworth. He hopes to soon enter the Tsenturion Brides program to find his own mate.

So, we all have our happy endings. And with Tsenturion Brides program, everyone else can have theirs too.

* * *

We invite you now to enter the Tsenturion Brides program.

Based on Medik and Frllil's ingenious system, we've created a series of books for all those who want to have a Tsenturion master. Your responses to this text have been recorded.

Rest assured that all potential Tsenturions Masters have thoroughly read the interspecies relationship manuals, including [Alien Captive], [Alien Tribute] and [Alien Abduction]. They are well practiced in the art of bride training. 😈

Our system has a 100% efficacy rate. Satisfaction guaranteed.

Click here to be added to the waiting list to be matched with an alien mate: https://www. subscribepage.com/tsenturionbridesprogram

ABOUT LEE SAVINO

Lee Savino is a USA today bestselling author of smexy romance. Smexy, as in "smart and sexy." Find her in the Goddess Group on facebook and download a free book at www.leesavino.com!

Find her at:
www.leesavino.com

Read on for an excerpt from Lee's Sci Fi Omegaverse with Tabitha Black

Brutal Mate

EXCERPT FROM BRUTAL MATE

KHAN

Spaceports always have a potent stench—the result of so many species crammed into a small space. I hold my breath against the stale reek of recycled air as I navigate the dark corridors on my way from my ship to the dark cantina. Only after I've settled at a table do I adjust my hood and take a careful inhale. The jumble of scents isn't always unpleasant. There are just so many smells all at once. No wonder my fellow Alphas prefer our home planet to space travel.

Today, the air is flavored with a thick musk from the Ogsul, the reptilian species running the auction. There are a million of them slinking around this spaceport. There's a hint of sulfur from a Buruwr, a giant, gelatinous creature sitting in its own trail of slime right in front of the auction stage. But underneath the overwhelming cacophony of smells, there's a delicate scent. Fragrant. Floral. Slightly musky.

The cantina is full of alien creatures, but no sign of what could produce such an amazing aroma. The perfume is growing stronger, like someone filled the room with a bouquet of blooms. But it's not a flower; it's a female. There are rumors of a special female to be found on the spaceport. That's why I'm here.

The stool creaks under me as I shift my weight. A few creatures glance my way and snap their gazes from mine. No one wants to catch the attention of an Ulfarri Alpha.

I rap the dinky table and, after a minute, a reluctant Ogsul trudges across the room with a drink for me.

"Brutal One." The Ogsul bows and leaves the smoking vat of my preferred fermented drink on the table beside me. I sniff but don't touch the oily liquid.

"Wait," I growl. A tremble runs up from his scaled tail to his hairy shoulders, but the Ogsul stops. "Tell me about the auction."

A pause. I don't have to negotiate or threaten. As an Alpha, my reputation precedes me. They call us the Brutal Ones for a reason.

"Sorry," the Ogsul says. "I get my chief." And he scurries away.

I settle back on the stool. The honey scent is growing heavier, sweeter. My canines ache, and my own rich scent is growing stronger in response.

Maybe the rumors are true. Maybe my travels across the galaxies have finally met with success. Maybe the time has come for me to find what I've been searching for all my life, what any Alpha would kill for: an Omega.

"Brutal One." Another Ogsul, this one taller with bulging eyes, appears at my table. He doesn't tremble but stands rigid, several lengths away. I beckon, and he takes a small step closer.

Close enough. I lean forward, keeping my face in shadow and my voice low. "Do you have the female?"

The thick black hair on his arms rises. "We have many females. For auction." His stumpy arm motions to the stage.

"But the…" If I say the word *Omega*, it's as good as shouting. "I heard you have something I want," I murmur.

Ahead and to my right, the giant, slug-like Buruwr quivers, more bitter-smelling goo leaking from it onto the floor. Creatures across the universe will pay to plant their seed in the Omega's fragrant, sacred womb. If the Buruwr wins the bid, it will take what is mine.

It will not win. I slide my hand down to stroke the hidden curve of my scimitar.

"There are tales that you have found what I am seeking. I am here, and I am willing to pay."

The creature's throat vibrates, a bitter scent pouring off his shaggy and scaly hide. But when I set a bag of coins on the table, his eyes bulge bigger.

"Yes," the Ogsul says, bobbing his head. "An Omega."

"You have one?" I forget myself and growl. The Ogsul leaps backwards a length faster than such a bulky creature should move. I curl my fist around my scimitar handle. "Where is the Omega? Tell me, now." I've searched long and far for a female to adequately replace the Omegas of my kind. So far, no luck.

"We prepare her. Auction."

"Is she Ulfarri?"

"No, Brutal One."

Damn. Probably some cow-titted creature. But a womb is a womb. And I want heirs.

"We have serum," he squeaks. "There is a creature we found that can take the Omega serum."

Interesting. I must learn more about this serum. But first… "Describe this creature."

"It called *Hoo-man.*" The Ogsul pulls out a holopad, and shows me a shadowy image. Not much to be seen but a small, frightened face surrounded by a mass of golden hair, peering out between the bars of a cage. Pale skin peeks out between shredded clothing.

"Frail," I sneer. "That will not satisfy me." I don't know this for sure. I won't know until I'm in a room with her. And if she is an Omega...

"It sentient," the Ogsul tells me. He takes a step forward, apparently overcoming his fear in his eagerness to make a sale. "Pretty. It won't disappoint."

"Fine." I feign boredom. "Show me."

The Ogsul's throat works up and down before he answers. "Auction soon."

I growl again, and the low murmur in the cantina is sucked away. "I do not wish to attend an auction," I say into the silence.

"Many creatures here to see the Hoo-man."

Hoo-man. I curl my tongue around the foreign word. This is another dead end. "Very well." I wave a hand, and the Ogsul bows and keeps bowing as he backs away. Like I've granted him a favor. Which I have. Maybe I won't kill anyone today.

My throat vibrates with a low growl. My hand tightens on the handle of my blade. I pride myself on my control, but there's one situation where even an Alpha struggles to keep control: the rut. When we're in heat, when we scent a sweet little Omega in the vicinity, even the most powerful Alphas are mindless.

And I'm as powerful as they come. I've fucked females of every size, shape, and species, and enjoyed most, but there's one type which has eluded me until now.

The sacred Omega.

My fated mate. The one female I was born to fuck.

Could this Hoo-man really be an Omega?

I lick my lips. The perfumed scent is thicker now. Still delicate and sweet, but growing in intensity. Is this the Hoo-man? My cock is awake, throbbing in my breeches.

The cantina is near packed now. Creatures stand between the tables, facing the stage. They've come to gawk over the pretty slaves of all different species, fitted with translation chips which will allow them to understand and speak any of the known languages, regardless of their own origin.

The Ogsul are a strange lot, but they do hold a good auction. I heard rumors they had a serum that could produce Omegas, but only now has that been verified. The last of the Omegas disappeared on Ulfaria a generation ago. If I can find one... I can breed her.

The Hoo-man was a pale, frail looking thing in the picture, but if she produces such perfume, I will buy her. And if anyone tries to bid higher, I will show them why my species, the Ulfarri, are called the Brutal Ones.

Perhaps this night will be more promising than I thought.

Getting to my feet, I take to the shadows, leaning back against the wall, crossing my arms. I'm tall enough to see easily over the heads of the other assembled males in the room. A wide variety of species have come to purchase a female, judging by the stinking males crowding this cantina. The small, cruel Rheeza, with their horned skulls and pointed noses. The docile, almost painfully shy Alags, with their four arms and purple skin. In the corner hunches a rare Haggat. So pale as to almost be translucent, his blazing third eye flicks back and forth over the assembled crowd of males, all of whom are apparently desperate for an Omega female.

They're all weaklings compared to me. Compared to the Alpha. I already pity the females they'll purchase. The one I choose—should I find the Hoo-man worthy—should be grateful she's escaped a much worse fate.

There's a screech, then a crackle, and then one of the Ogsul plods onto the stage. He's holding a microphone and looking enormously pleased with himself.

"Gentlemen, thank you for traveling such long way," he begins in his thick, guttural language. He seems to have a much broader vocabulary than most of the Ogsul I've met before. "As always, we have a fine array of females for you to choose from, so please be generous in your bids." He hesitates, then hums and leans forward. "I'm especially pleased to be able to tell you that we have one of the rarest kinds of females on offer for you tonight." He pauses for effect again before continuing. "An Omega."

There's a hum of excitement traveling around the room, and I know that every other male is thinking the same thing I am:

That Omega will be mine.

The noxious stench in the room thickens as the dozens of males lean forward, eager to get a glimpse of the first female slave for sale. I duck my head further in my hood to gain a little reprieve from the blend of sweat and testosterone. No trace of the sweet floral scent from earlier, the perfect honey scent like light on my tongue. Curse my sensitive sense of smell. I should have brought a breathing mask. Thank Ulf I'm not in rut, else I'd be gagging by now.

"First female on offer is number 327, a shy little Tyreen!"

There's a deep rumble of lowered voices as the obviously petrified slave is shoved unceremoniously onstage. She has thick black hair falling in waves down to her knees, her dress is torn, and all six of her nipples are clearly visible through the sheer fabric. I can almost sense her trembling from my position at the back of the room. Leaning forward, I inhale deeply, concentrating in order to separate her scent from the other smells in the room. There's definitely an underlying trace of sweetness, but it doesn't stir me. I lean back and fold my arms once more.

A female with six breasts and pale lilac skin will always garner attention from some males, and there are a flurry of bids being roared from one end of the room to the other. At length, the Tyreen is sold to a great beast of a Dajok, who has difficulty hiding his smug grin as he strides toward the stage to claim his new slave.

One after another, females of all kinds are led onto the wooden platform, all of them in various states of undress. Some look petrified, others look mutinous. But they're all sold, regardless. There is no escape. That is the way of the universe.

I fondle the handle of my scimitar. It's been ages, and there's still no sign of the promised Hoo-man. The stench of so many species crammed into a small space is thick enough to cut. I still have plenty of competition. Only the wealthiest and most powerful would stand a chance at winning her, so the males of lesser species are contenting themselves with the other goods on offer. Most of them have already collected their new purchases and left, so I have a clear over-view of the males I must beat in order to make the rare jewel mine.

"And now, saving the best for last, I'm proud to present the promised Omega! A Hoo-man!" the Ogsul host announces.

As the evening's highlight is propelled onstage, the remaining males lean forward as one, myself included.

So, this is a Hoo-man. She's smaller than I anticipated—a lot smaller. Pale pink skin, two arms, two legs, two breasts. But the cloud of tousled hair around her head is a glittering gold, her eyes are huge and innocent and, when her rich, honeyed perfume hits my nostrils, I bite back a roar as the rut grips me with no warning; no preamble.

Suddenly, my cock is rock solid and pounding, my skin prickles, and my pulse is thudding in my ears.

I'm no longer able to form a coherent thought. My entire being screams just one thing:

She will be mine.

READ BRUTAL MATE NOW!

Check out all Lee's sci fi Omegaverse romance (co-written with Tabitha Black)

Brutal Mate
Brutal Claim
Brutal Capture
Brutal Beast

Sci Fi Omegaverse romance with Tabitha Black

Brutal Mate

Brutal Claim

Brutal Capture

Brutal Beast

More Possessive Warrior Sci fi romance

Draekon Rebel Force with Lili Zander

Start with Draekon Warrior

Ménage Sci Fi Romance

Draekons (Dragons in Exile) with Lili Zander (ménage alien dragons)

Crashed spaceship. Prison planet. Two big, hulking, bronzed aliens who turn into dragons. The best part? The dragons insist I'm their mate.

Paranormal romance

Love growly alphas? Check out the Berserker Saga. Start with Sold to the Berserkers.

And the Bad Boy Alphas with Renee Rose (bad boy werewolves)

Never ever date a werewolf.

ABOUT GOLDEN ANGEL

Angel is an international best-selling BDSM and interracial romance author and self-described bibliophile with a "kinky" bent who loves to write stories for the characters in her head. If she didn't get them out, she's pretty sure she'd go just a little crazy.

She is happily married, old enough to know better but still too young to care, and a big fan of happily-ever-afters, strong heroes and heroines, and sizzling chemistry.

She believes the world is a better place when there's a little magic in it.

Sign up for the Angel Legion newsletter here - https://mailchi.mp/9eb82a414844/angelnewsletter - and grab several FREE sexy stories immediately in a welcome message!

Read on for an excerpt from her alien romance, Mated on Hades…

EXCERPT: MATED ON HADES

"Welcome to your new home for the next four twenty-cycles," he said, stepping aside so she could enter the cabin behind him, his tone dryly sarcastic. "As you can see, you would have been better off with my parents."

Rather than telling him that the room was about the size of her entire living space back on Earth—and unlike her home there, this room wasn't crammed with equipment—Jules just looked around as she walked past him. Sparsely furnished, the massive bed on the far wall dominated the whole area. It was even bigger than the bed in her room at Tobik and Sirilla's, and she'd thought *that* was huge.

Turning around, she enjoyed the disgruntled look on Tarrik's face as he set her bag down next to the open closet door. Since his clothing seemed to consist mostly of pants and a kind of tunic vest that she'd seen on a lot of winged Hadesians, there was plenty of space for her meager belongings.

"This looks great," she said. "As long as you keep to your side of the bed."

Now his expression was almost infuriated. "Of course I will. I'm not the one who can't keep her hands to herself."

"Excuse me?" Jules' hands slammed onto her hips as she glared back at him. "Since when have I not kept my hands to myself?"

"Uh, that would be last night when you kissed me."

She gaped. "You kissed me!"

"I sure as hell did not," he snapped back. "I'm not even attracted to you."

"Is that why your cock was digging a hole in my stomach last night when *you kissed me*?"

"Look, just stay on whichever side of the bed you pick, keep your hands to yourself, and this trip will be over before you know it."

Jules was still sputtering and trying to find a good retort as he swept out of the room. *Jerk!* She couldn't believe she'd let him have the last word.

"Stupid butt monkey," she muttered, flopping back onto the bed just to see how it felt. It was ridiculously comfortable of course. Which only made her more irritated with him for some reason, even though he had nothing to do with it.

He'd definitely kissed her first.

At the very least, they'd kissed each other.

Her lips pursed as a wicked idea occurred to her. It would be playing with fire a little bit... but on the other hand, he definitely deserved it. And it would be even more amusing than keeping his ship grounded until her say so.

Just as that thought flickered through her mind, she felt the reverberations of the ship as it began to blast off. Excitement surged. She, Jules, who had never even thought she would see planet other than Earth, was now on her second spaceship this week and off to see a whole *bunch* of planets.

While part of her couldn't help but wonder what was happening back on Earth, if anyone was helping those in need, another part of her was thrilled to be on an adventure. New places, new beings, new things to see and do... If this was how traveling made Tarrik feel, no wonder he didn't want to give it up.

As soon as she thought it, she scowled. She didn't want to feel sympathy for him dammit.

Pushing any thoughts of the alien male aside, Jules made herself get up from the bed and start unpacking. The sooner she was done, the sooner she could explore the ship.

* * *

THE SYSTEMS WERE RUNNING PERFECTLY, the entire crew was happy, and Tarrik was feeling a lot better than he'd expected. The only thing that would make this trip better was if Juliette wasn't on board.

Not that she was in the way. No, she was entirely helpful, going out of her way to make herself useful.

Tarrik told himself he wasn't jealous over the way she and Mrik had obviously bonded. They definitely weren't behaving as though they were sexually attracted to each other—Tarrik knew that Mrik would never move on Tarrik's female regardless—but he still got a gnawing feeling in his stomach when he saw them laughing together. It might be more envy than jealousy though... she definitely didn't smile at him that way or laugh with him...

Not that he'd given her any reason to.

Because I don't want to, he reminded himself for the umpteenth time. The problem was that saying it wasn't making it true.

She was beautiful when she smiled. Engaging when she laughed. The rest of the crew definitely liked her, she'd already made fast friends with his maintenance engineers, Lessys and Sasslys, who were both Vloss and mated to each other. When they asked if Juliette had ever seen anything like them before, she said they looked like miniature Godzillas, without the back plates. The whole crew found this hysterical when Myrik looked up what she was speaking of.

So he wasn't in the best mood by bedtime.

His mood got a hell of a lot worse when he laid down and Juliette announced she was going to take a shower.

"Great," he said. And then nearly choked when she started undressing right in the middle of the bedroom. She pulled her shirt over her head, revealing tanned skin, soft mounds of her breasts filling out her feminine support, a gently rounded stomach that he suddenly ached to draw his tongue over... When she began tugging down her pants, he finally managed to find his voice again even if it did sound like he was being strangled when he spoke. "What the gark are you doing?"

Juliette glanced at him and he bit back a groan as her pants slid to the ground, revealing muscled legs and tight-fitting panties. The white underwear wasn't the sexiest he'd ever seen, it was more utilitarian than anything else, and yet he found he couldn't look away. The temperature in the room seemed to have risen by a few degrees and his tail was lashing back and forth furiously as his cock started to swell.

"I'm taking a shower," she said, blinking at him like he'd said something incomprehensible.

"The shower is in there." Pointing to the facilities, he shifted slightly to hopefully cover up his growing erection.

"Why do you care?" she asked, pulling off her support garment. Tarrik almost whimpered as her rounded, full breasts were revealed, perfectly sized to fit in his palm, with tightly ruched brown nipples just begging for attention. His erection swelled to fullness and his tail had taken on a mind of its own—any attempt to control it was useless. "You're not attracted to me, remember?"

Turning, she bent at the waist to pull her undergarments down, giving him a glorious view of her ass before she sauntered into the bathroom.

Closing his eyes didn't help in the least. The image of her naked body was burned into his retinas. Gark it, he didn't even *want* to forget.

When he heard the water turn on, he did groan, because now all he could think about was the hot water sluicing over her body, caressing her skin the way he wanted to.

Garking...

Laying back in the bed, Tarrik jerked off the tunic he was going to sleep in out of respect for her. Immediately he fisted his hand around his shaft and groaned as he began to pump, closing his eyes and picturing her rounded bottom and the little smirk on her lips... the way the water would slide over her breasts and stomach and down between her legs... he hadn't gotten nearly as close a look of *that* as he'd wanted to.

He'd seen images of nude human females though, and his feverish brain extrapolated for him.

Wet flesh, ripe and ready for him.

He pumped his cock harder, faster as he imagined her bent over for him, the way she had taken off her underwear, his hand slapping against her ass as he pounded into her from behind, his tail twining around her breasts...

He wanted her *bad*.

Pleasure surged and his *jimen* spurted, sticky and hot onto his stomach, leaving him only slightly less wound up.

* * *

WAS HE... WAS HE MASTURBATING? JULES' paused as she washed her hair, her body flushing as she heard another low masculine groan, just barely audible to her. Yeah, so much for not being attracted to her.

Of course, she was very much in the same boat. Just stripping down in front of him had given her a little thrill. She'd never known she had a little bit of exhibitionist in her, but she'd definitely gotten turned on feeling his eyes sliding over her naked skin with every article of clothing she'd peeled off. It had made her feel freaking sexy.

Knowing he was out there jerking off after the little show she'd put on...

Well that just made her feel even sexier.

It didn't help that she hadn't gotten laid in... geez, it had been months since her last encounter with the male kind. So she also had a lot of pent-up sexual energy to work off.

Her hands moved over her body, slick and soapy, touching her hard nipples and massaging her breasts before moving down her stomach. Leaning back against the cool wall, she kept one hand on her breast while the other slipped between her pussy lips. Biting her lip to keep her own moans quiet, she closed her eyes and pictured him coming into the bathroom, watching her touch herself...

Then he wouldn't be able to stay back. He'd step in, crowding her in the shower, his body hot and hard against hers as he lifted her up, and she'd wrap her legs around his waist as she slid down his body and right onto his hard cock.

Shuddering, Jules managed to keep her noises to heavy breathing as she rubbed out a hard, fast orgasm that took the edge off but didn't completely satisfy her. She didn't want to take too long in the shower though; she definitely didn't want him to think she was in here getting off to him... the same way she was pretty sure he was getting off to her.

Stepping out of the shower, Jules quickly dried off and went into the main cabin. The lights were already dim and Tarrik was on his side of the bed, the sheets pulled up to his waist and he'd built a wall of cushions down the center of the bed. His muscled chest and arms were clearly visible—he'd taken off his tunic and it lay in a crumpled heap on the floor. Had he been wearing anything else? Or was he naked under the sheet?

Don't think about that!

In the dark, her body thrumming with sexual frustration, Jules was no closer to sleep than she had been when the lights had been turned on. Despite the wall of cushions between them, she was far, far too aware of the insanely sexy alien on the bed with her, less than a foot of distance separating them. How much body heat did a Hadesian emanate? Because she swore she could feel him.

Then she really did feel something, touching her ankle between the sheets, and she shrieked, kicking.

"Sorry, sorry!" Tarrik's deep voice actually sounded sincere. "That was my tail, sorry."

Jules' heart pounded so hard it felt like it was going to go right out of her chest as her fear of the unknown settled.

"Well get your tail under control," she hissed at him, pulling her legs up slightly, closer to her body and telling herself that she definitely was not going to think about the possibilities of a tail that had a mind of its own.

"It's not exactly easy," he hissed back. "I can *smell* your arousal. So don't bother lying and telling me that you aren't."

Heat flushed her cheeks and she was very glad the room was dark enough that he wouldn't be able to see her blush. "That's just a physical response—and you were the one who started jerking off while I was in the shower!"

"You stripped down in front of me!"

"*You* said you weren't attracted to me!"

"I lied, alright?!" There was a strange ominous red glow in the darkness and suddenly cushions went flying. Tarrik loomed over her, wings spread slightly in his agitation. Holy fracking radiation. He freaking glowed in the dark. "I'm attracted to you, okay? That doesn't mean I want to mate you."

"I don't want to mate you either, you overgrown ignoramus."

"But you want to *fuck* me, right?" From the way he said 'fuck', she could tell he'd looked up the human word at some point but that it wasn't terminology he was used to. The glow of his skin brightened a little more, illuminating her body as he taunted her, his own sexual frustration clear on his face. It was eerie and sexy all at the same time and this time when his tail curled around her ankle, the heat of his flesh warming her skin, she didn't jump or kick.

"Oh shut up and do something useful with your mouth," she snarled back, reaching up to grab his face and pull his lips down to meet hers.

MATED ON HADES

*T*he Celestial Mates agency always knows what - or who - you need.

TARRIK WOULD DO anything to avoid breaking his mother's heart, so he begrudgingly signs up for Celestial Mates and agrees to come home and settle down once the agency finds his match. There's just one catch: he's not ready to give up his free and easy life traveling the galaxy. And he's doing exactly as his mother asked, so what will it hurt if he makes himself as unappealing as possible on his mate application?

JULIETTE IS a woman on the run. Her attitude, and more importantly her hacking skills, have pissed off all the wrong people. Now the target of a contract hit, she's decided the solution to her problems is to leave the planet as fast as she can. The Celestial Mates program is exactly what she needs. By the time her "mate" realizes she's impossible to live with, hopefully it will be safe for her to return to earth. She wasn't counting on a seriously hot alien who looked like the devil and could do the most sinful things with his tail...

THE SPARKS FLY at first meeting when their chemistry ignites. But they can barely stand to be in the same room with each other.

THEY SHOULDN'T WORK AT ALL.

BUT CELESTIAL MATES always knows best.